HAYWIRED

By Alex Keller

MOGZILLA

HAYWIRED

First published by Mogzilla in 2010

Paperback edition:
ISBN: 978-1-906132-33-0

Text copyright Alex Keller 2009
Cover by Rachel de Ste. Croix
Cover ©Mogzilla 2010
Copy editor: Mogzilla
Printed in Malta

http://www.mogzilla.co.uk/haywired

http://alexkelleruk.tumblr.com/

Chapter One:
It Begins

In the gardens of Castle Guggenstein, a young boy of no more than eleven or twelve strolled over to a cannon sitting on the well-kept lawn.

Next to the cannon was Mr Shawlworth. The old castle gardener stood peering over his half moon spectacles, trying to make sense of a piece of paper in his hands. 'Ah Ludwig,' he said, looking up. 'Ready?'

The boy called Ludwig nodded. 'Sure. What do you want me to do?'

'We're going for a field half a mile away this time. Can you lift the cannon -five degrees...'

Ludwig bent down and tilted the cannon until its dial read forty-five. 'Done.'

'Now, drop in the pod.'

On the ground near Ludwig's feet was a round metal ball about the size of a man's fist. He picked it up and shook it. Inside he could hear seeds bouncing around. He dropped it into the barrel and listened to it roll down, hitting the bottom with a satisfying clunk. 'And done,' he called over his shoulder.

'Good. Now you best stand back. Your dad'll have my head if you get hurt again,' said the gardener.

Ludwig stood next to one of the flowerbeds and watched as Mr Shawlworth stepped up to the cannon.

The gardener looked at the paper in his hand once more. 'It says I have to...' He reached out and a low hum came from the cannon, followed by a rumbling that slowly grew louder. Then the ground began to shake.

'Is it meant to do that?' Ludwig asked uncertainly.

'Definitely,' said the gardener, not sounding very definite at all. 'And when this dial gets to a hundred I have to press…ah!' Mr Shawlworth hit one of the bigger buttons and jumped away, diving into a ball and covering his head with his hands. However, after a few moments of silence, he peered up to see Ludwig standing looking unconcerned.

Nothing had happened.

'It hasn't worked,' said Ludwig.

Mr Shawlworth began to get up. 'Well, at least it didn't–'

BOOOOOOMMMMMM!!!!

The explosion was tremendous. A great gust of wind knocked the gardener face down again with a grunt. 'Agh! Hellfire!' he cried, covering his head as clods of earth and shards of metal crashed into the lawn around him.

Ludwig, meanwhile, had found himself lying in the flowerbed covered in petals. He wiped the flowers from his face and looked up to see the metal pod shooting up into the sky at an incredible speed, clipping the side of the castle on its way.

'Your father's not going to like this,' said Mr Shawlworth when the ringing in his ears had died down. He looked at the hole that had been left in the ground. 'And that's going to be a right nightmare to sort out.'

Ludwig sat up. 'At least it fired in the right direction this time,' he said.

Mr Shawlworth shrugged and pulled out his pocket watch. 'You need to go, lad, you've got your lessons.'

Ludwig got up, nodded, and, swaying slightly, made his way back inside the squat castle he called home.

This was how many of his mornings began.

In the kitchens, Ludwig found Mrs Pewsnitt, the castle housekeeper, washing the breakfast dishes. Her husband sat at the table with a cup of tea in one hand and the paper in the other. He usually popped in to visit his wife at this hour. Father didn't mind. They both looked up when he opened the door.

'Morning love,' Mrs Pewsnitt cooed. She passed Ludwig a freshly-made bacon sandwich, which he took gratefully. 'Nothing broken this morning I 'ope?'

'No,' said Ludwig shaking his head. He slid onto a chair, dropped his plate on the table, and started on his breakfast.

'All right, lad?' said Mr Pewsnitt. 'How goes the new thingumabob? We 'eard Arthur cursing all the way in here, as well as the explosion of course.'

Ludwig mumbled something between mouthfuls and Mr Pewnitt looked at him oddly. 'Nothing to worry about,' Ludwig finally managed. 'Thanks Mrs Pewsnitt!' he got up and ran out of the room.

'Strange lad,' said Mr Pewsnitt before returning to his paper.

Ludwig made his way through Castle Guggenstein's great hall and up the staircase that led to its library. Behind the library doors he could hear the faint sound of music that meant his father was inside. Opening one, he stepped through.

The library was vast. Row upon row of bookcases led away from the main doors, each one crammed from floor to ceiling with books of every possible size and length. Ancient myths sat next to astronomy that sat next to advanced mathematics and music theory, all jumbled together in no apparent order. Ludwig wandered between the books towards the light at the end of the main aisle. Soon enough, the shelves ended and the room opened up to a space in which stood an old desk, a comfortable leather chair, and to one side, an odd-looking piano.

At the odd-looking piano sat his father.

Mandrake von Guggenstein had his eyes closed when Ludwig arrived. He was tall, and like Ludwig, dark and thin. At this precise moment he sat with his shoulders straight and his head tilted slightly to one side as his long fingers danced across the piano's keys, lost in his music and seemingly totally unaware of his son standing nearby.

Until...

'My boy,' Mandrake said gently over the melody. 'Did our cannon perform its duties admirably?'

'Well...' mumbled Ludwig. 'Not exactly.'

'Hmm?'

'It left a hole in the garden and we're not sure where the pod went; but at least it *fired* this time.'

Mandrake sighed. 'Ah, that's better than yesterday at least. Oh well, it can't be helped; we are scientists after all and mistakes will be made.' He dropped the piano cover, walked over to one of the shelves and took a book, not bothering to check the spine. 'Now, sit down and we will begin.'

Ludwig climbed into the chair behind the desk and waited.

'Magdaliana's *Metallugica*,' Mandrake said, tapping his hand on the book and pushing it under Ludwig's nose. 'We'll continue from page two hundred and thirteen.'

Ludwig flicked to the right page and cast his eye over complex signs and patterns. Then he took a pencil and waited while his father cleared his throat.

'Ludwig,' said his father later that day, 'We'll finish here for now. Put your books away.'

Ludwig cleared his things and got up, but as he made his way back to the kitchen for lunch, his father called him back.

'I'm not quite done with you yet.'

Ludwig smiled. 'It's ready?' he asked.

His father didn't reply. Instead, he pulled out a piece of paper from his jacket pocket and pinned it to the desk with a couple of paperweights.

Ludwig went over and looked down. It *was* the new project. 'What about the cannon?' he asked.

'We can put it to one side for awhile. This is far more important.'

The thing on the paper was human-shaped, with two arms and two legs attached to a round, stocky body. The machine's head was pushed forward so its top was at the same level as its shoulders, and on its head was nothing more than two bulbous, glassy lumps, like the eyes of a fly. Overall, the whole thing looked like an overweight praying mantis.

'What is it?' Ludwig asked.

'An Heuristic Engine with Learning and Obedience Tailoring,' replied his father.

'A what?'

'It's a bit of a mouthful I know, so I've called it the HELOT for short.'

Ludwig looked over the design. 'What does it do?'

'Let me show you.'

His father leaned over the desk and flicked a switch. There was a buzzing sound followed by the clattering of dishes. 'Mrs Pewsnitt, can you hear me?' Mandrake called out.

'Loud an' clear, sir. No problem! What can I do for yer?' came the voice of the housekeeper.

'Could you be so kind as to bring us our lunch in the library today?'

'Right you are dear!' The radio went silent.

Mandrake took his son by the shoulders, turned him so he was facing the doors, and lent down to speak in his ear. 'Now watch.'

A minute later, the library doors opened. Mrs Pewsnitt came in with a silver tray in her hands. She let out a sigh and slowly made her way to Ludwig and his father, careful not to drop anything.

'Where would you like it, sir?' she asked politely.

'On the desk please,' replied Mandrake.

Mrs Pewsnitt put the tray down and rubbed her back. 'Oh that's better,' she muttered. Suddenly she glanced at Ludwig and his father as if she'd forgotten they were there, then quickly took her hands away from her back. She looked embarrassed. 'You've got pork, potatoes, and veg. Plus a glass of wine for you, sir, and water for Ludwig, of course.'

'Thank you Mrs Pewsnitt,' said Mandrake.

'Anything else dears?'

'No. This will be more than adequate I'm sure.'

Ludwig just shook his head.

'Right you are,' she finished and hobbled away out of the library, closing the door quietly behind her.

'What did you notice boy?' Ludwig's father asked when the housekeeper was gone.

Ludwig was silent.

'Come on. What struck you?'

'Well, she's getting old...'

Mandrake patted his son on the back. 'Exactly. Did you see the way she moved? The effort? She's getting frail boy, and it's not just Mrs Pewsnitt. I think it's time to take the next step in our work.'

'You're going to replace her?' asked Ludwig, fearfully.

'No,' said his father, his eyes bright, 'We're going to *help* her.'

Chapter Two:
Sir Notsworth O'Reilly

The months passed quickly as father and son worked on the HELOT. Each morning they would rise early and, after breakfast, disappear into the workshop for the rest of the day. Mrs Pewsnitt rarely saw them until dinner.

Then, one spring afternoon, Ludwig wiped his brow and pulled the blowtorch away from a leg joint he was welding. He took a step back and admired his work. 'It's nearly done!' he called out.

His father looked up from the clockwork innards across the room. 'Not long now.'

Just as Ludwig was about to turn the torch back on and get back to work, a loud chime echoed through the castle. 'Someone's at the door!' he cried in surprise.

'Were you expecting anyone?' asked his father, quietly.

Ludwig shook his head. 'No.'

'Neither was I.'

Ludwig rushed from the workshop and got to the main hall just in time to see Mrs Pewsnitt pull the lever that opened the front gates. Then she wobbled over to the heavy front doors and pulled them open. At this angle Ludwig couldn't see who had arrived, but the deep, booming voice that greeted the housekeeper was enough. He grinned.

'Mrs Pewsnitt!' the voice behind the door bellowed. 'Such a picture of loveliness as I ever saw!'

Ludwig watched the house keeper's face flush.

'Oh Sir, get away with yer!' she said, fanning herself with her hand. 'Come in! Come in! I'll call the Professor.'

'Thank you, my dear, but I'd like to surprise him myself. Is he in the library?'

'No sir, the workshop.'

'Hard at work eh? Excellent. I shall go to him forthwith.'

But before the man had taken two steps, he stopped as he caught sight of Ludwig bounding across the hall.

'Notsworth!' Ludwig cried.

The man's eyes lit up and he let out a great laugh. 'Ludwig! My boy! It's been far, far too long!'

Ludwig jumped up and wrapped his arms around the guest. The man threw him up into the air and caught him again before setting him down on the ground and looking him over.

'Well, you've grown lad and no mistake. How have you been? Not causing too much trouble for Mrs Pewsnitt here, I hope?'

Mrs Pewsnitt tittered and denied any wrongdoing while the big man waited for Ludwig to reply, but Ludwig was too excited to speak. The man chuckled, bent down, then pulled his shoulder bag round to his front and began to rummage inside.

'I think I might have something here for you,' he said, taking his time to go through the bag's contents. He began pulling out one strange item after another, only to put it back in his bag again with a shake of his head. 'No, that's not it,' he said rummaging again. 'No. It must be here somewhere...'

'Notsworth, please!' Ludwig moaned.

The man looked up at Ludwig and gave him a wink. 'Ah! Here we go!'

He pulled out his hand once more, and between his fingers was an oblong shape wrapped in brown paper, tied with an ordinary piece of string. Ludwig grabbed the package and tore the paper away, letting the string fall to the floor still knotted. The man looked on and laughed.

Inside was a book. Ludwig read the title: *The Travels of Sir Notsworth O'Reilly, Adventurer: Vol. XIII.* 'You've finished it!' he cheered. 'I've been waiting so long! Thank you!'

Ludwig looked at the picture on the cover. There stood Sir Notsworth O'Reilly, dressed in his explorer's uniform, with one hand on his waist and the other holding a huge elephant gun. Under one foot was a giant white tiger; its eyes closed and its paws crossed underneath its head. Ludwig pointed at the beast.

'Is that Abberati?'

'Of course. She looks really dead, doesn't she? You should have seen the artist's face when I told him he had to paint her! I nearly had to nail his feet to the floor!'

Ludwig opened the book and flicked through the pages. As he read, he didn't notice the footsteps behind him. He jumped when his father spoke.

'You spoil the boy, Notsworth.'

Notsworth stood up and grinned. 'Bah, I don't spoil him enough.' He rubbed Ludwig's hair with one hand and then walked over to Mandrake with the other out-stretched. 'Greetings, old man.'

Mandrake took his hand and shook it. 'A pleasure, Notsworth, as always. Will you be staying for dinner?'

'Do you have to ask?' Notsworth replied.

The dining room of the castle was only used for special occasions, but when those occasions arrived, the best silver was laid out, the candles lit, and Mrs Pewsnitt put a lot of extra effort into her meals. A visit from Sir Notsworth O'Reilly could certainly be considered special.

Sitting at the table, Ludwig tried to force just one more piece of lamb into his mouth while he thumbed through

Notsworth's book, ignoring the disapproving looks from his father. The explorer sat next to him and Ludwig bombarded him with questions at every opportunity. He only saw Sir Notsworth O'Reilly once a year at best despite him being his father' closest friend, and any opportunity to get him to tell his stories was not to be missed.

'And then what happened?' Ludwig asked excitedly.

'As I ran down into the valley, I knew I was in trouble,' replied Sir Notsworth. 'Fortunately, I'd managed to lose the beasts that had been trailing me all night, but supplies were running low and things were getting worrying. On top of that, I could see a storm brewing...'

Ludwig didn't look impressed. Wild animals were scary, weather wasn't.

'Nothing like what you get here,' Sir Notsworth exclaimed. 'The storms in Hryic are brute things! Raindrops that'll leave a dent in your head! Wind that'll sweep you off your feet and over the nearest cliff!' He waved a chicken leg around his head to show the massiveness of the storm. 'So I pulled out the old telescope and took a peek around. Down below, I spied a group of huts. Ah ha! I thought to myself, this could be promising. I'd heard rumours the tribes around here weren't overly keen on strangers, but needs must and all that.'

Ludwig nodded keenly.

'So I made my way down the hillside, all battered and bruised, and got to a village more dead than alive. I caught sight of a few natives and begged them for a bite to eat and a place to keep out of the storm—'

'And they helped?'

'If only! They took one look at me and started screaming! A few minutes later all their chums had come out to join the fun, spears and all. I thought I was a goner! But with whatever strength I had left, I made a run for it. It was a close thing, but thank Azmon there was a river not too far away. I made my way to it post haste and jumped in, hoping the current would carry me somewhere a bit less threatening.'

'Didn't they follow you?'

'No lad. I think they were put off by the hundred-foot drop! As I always say, possible death is better than certain death. So I jumped and they didn't, and I live to tell the tale.' The big man leaned back, looking rather happy with himself.

Ludwig smiled. 'Is that where you've just come from?'

'Oh no, I got back from Hryic months ago. I've been on government business since then.' Notsworth lent close and tapped his finger to his nose. 'All very hush hush.'

'And how *are* our fearless leaders?' asked Mandrake, suddenly more interested in the conversation.

'Well enough,' replied Notsworth. 'They're the reason I'm here if I'm honest with you.'

'Oh?'

'Indeed, old man.' Notsworth paused and looked uncomfortable. 'Look, we need to have a little chat.'

Ludwig's father let out a sigh. 'What do they want *this* time Notsworth? I'm rather busy. I assume the war is going well.'

'Well old chap, about that... There have been a few developments...'

Mandrake's eyes narrowed. 'Go on.'

Notsworth set down his knife and fork, and then unbuttoned the top of his shirt. 'Look, to make a long story short, it looks like the war's coming to an end. Good news eh?'

Mandrake said nothing. Then he got up and quietly spoke to Ludwig. 'Could you excuse yourself, my boy. I must talk to Notsworth alone. There may be words.'

'But I want to know what happened!" Ludwig replied.

'It wasn't a request, Ludwig. Leave. Now.'

Ludwig was about to argue, but the look on his father's face made him stop. 'Fine,' he said quietly.

Back in his room, Ludwig climbed onto his bed and thought about what Notsworth had said. *The war is coming to an end?* And to be sent away just as the conversation was getting interesting, it was infuriating! The war between Pallenway and Galleesha had been going on for as long as Ludwig could remember. Each day there were reports in the newspaper saying Pallenway had taken this town or Galleesha had defeated that army. Thousands of lives had been lost.

Ludwig huffed angrily and looked over to his night stand. On it was Notsworth's book. He picked it up again and started reading to take his mind off what was going on downstairs. However, as he turned the pages, something distracted him. He looked up, searching the room. He thought he could hear a slight sound coming from one corner. It was faint, on the edge of hearing, but definitely there. He put the book down and got up off his bed, following the sound over to the chest of drawers on the other side of his room.

As Ludwig got nearer the sound became clearer, and by the time he got to the drawers he was sure he knew what it was. He could hear his father and Notsworth talking!

He bent down to try to look behind the drawers. There was a glint in the darkness! He was sure of it. Something metallic shone down there. Ludwig moved the things from the top of the drawers onto the floor, and then he put his fingers to the drawers' edge closest to the wall and pulled. The drawers were heavy, but with a few strong tugs they came away. Behind, he found a metal grating. Warm air came out of it along with the voices.

They're in father's study, thought Ludwig. *No-one is allowed in there, ever...* He lowered himself down and listened.

'Our "great" government. Those cowards!' Ludwig heard his father cry, 'No spine and no pride. I should petition for their removal!'

'Steady on old chap!' came Notsworth's voice. 'Saying things like that could get you in front of a judge in other company!'

'They're a failure, Notsworth. Completely and utterly.'

'But–'

'A failure! And Galleesha! That abominable country needs to be wiped off the map! If I had my way it would be nothing but dust and cinders by now.'

'We barely remember what we're fighting for anymore Mandrake. Be reasonable.'

'I know *exactly* why I'm fighting.'

'Anyway...' said Notsworth, sounding to Ludwig like he was trying to change the subject. 'The boy looks fine.'

'What?' said Mandrake distractedly. 'Yes, yes, he's doing extremely well.'

'Last time I saw him I think he barely came up to my knee! Bright too by the sound of it.'

'Did you expect anything less?'

'Of course not old man, not with you at the helm.'

'Indeed.'

There was a short uncomfortable silence.

'No... problems then?'

A pause.

'How do you mean?'

'Well, you know. What with Hephaestus and all that... nothing untoward has occurred I hope.'

Mandrake relaxed. 'No. He appears as any child should.'

'Oh, that's good.'

Ludwig heard his father sigh. 'Hephaestus was such a shame. So much promise. If only I could have helped him before... well, it's in the past now.'

'These things happen. You weren't to know.'

'But still...'

'Ludwig will be fine I'm sure.'

'Of course. He hasn't been affected, thankfully.'

'Have you told him yet?'

'No. He doesn't need to know. His brother was the past. It's best for him if he never finds out.'

From somewhere near the roof there was a loud gasp. Both men looked at each other.

'Ah,' said Notsworth.

Ludwig fell back from the grate and sat down heavily. He stared at the opposite wall, stunned.

Minutes later, his bedroom door burst open and his father stepped in. Mandrake took one look at the grate and the pulled out drawers, then another at Ludwig.

'I have a brother?' said Ludwig.

'Boy, you know better than to eavesdrop on other people's conversations.'

'I have a *brother*!?'

His father walked over and sat down beside him. '"Had", I'm afraid,' he said softly. 'Oh child, I didn't want you to find out like this.'

'You weren't going to tell me at all. You just said so.'

'No. I wasn't.'

'Why?'

'Because...' His father's eyes wandered around the room.

'Because I thought it would upset you. You had a brother but he passed away a long time ago. Why should I burden you with the loss of someone you never even knew? Telling you didn't seem to matter.'

Ludwig looked at his father. 'I deserved to know anyway.'

'Perhaps,' his father replied. 'I wasn't trying to be deceitful, but what with your mother...' he put his hand on Ludwig's arm. 'I'm sorry.'

Mandrake was about to get up when Ludwig caught his jacket.

'What happened to him?'

'He suffered from a terrible disease that wracked his body. He didn't live long. It was always a concern that you may suffer too, but thankfully it looks like you are well. And you're much older than he was when he passed.'

Ludwig was silent. His father stood up and placed a hand on his son's head before quietly leaving the room.

Chapter Three:
The Accident

When Ludwig got up the next day, it wasn't the alarm that woke him. Instead, he found his father at the end of his bed with a mug of warm milk in his hands, the steam whirling up towards the ceiling.

'How are you feeling?' Mandrake asked, passing his son the milk.

Ludwig took it and drank. It felt warm as it slid down his throat. 'I'm okay,' he replied quietly.

'Good.' His father rose and brushed the creases from his trousers. 'Come with me, boy. I have something to show you. Notsworth left early this morning. He apologises for not saying goodbye, but he felt we should be alone after last night. This is just between us.'

Ludwig got out of bed and put on some clothes. His father led him from his bedroom downstairs to the workshop. In the workshop, Ludwig was left near the doorway while his father walked over to one corner of the room, to a spot where something was covered with an old sheet.

Mandrake glanced back to make sure Ludwig was watching, and then pulled the cover away. Underneath stood the HELOT. 'What do you think?' he asked.

'You finished it! When?'

'Last night. Notsworth went to bed and I came here. It was almost complete so I just put it all together.'

Ludwig rushed over to get a better look. It was an ugly little thing, like a bizarre statue. It stood absolutely still.

'Why isn't it working?' he asked.

'Ah,' replied Mandrake. 'Let me show you something.' He went over to one of the work benches, pulled open a drawer, and carefully took something out which he hid behind his back. He came back to Ludwig and brought his hands out in front of him.

'Because it doesn't have this.'

Ludwig stared at the thing in his father's hands. It was a small metal cube, maybe three inches or so wide and the same high, with raised lines all across its surfaces made of a different material. Small holes covered with glass were placed here and there on some of the cube's sides. Peering down, Ludwig could see lights blinking on and off in some of the holes and a pale constant glow from others. He went to pick the cube up but to his surprise, his father quickly pulled it out of his reach.

'No boy. It's too fragile.'

'What is it?' Ludwig asked.

'It's a counting device of sorts,' Mandrake replied, his eyes fixed on the thing in his hands. 'It harnesses certain energies and turns them into commands for the HELOT to obey. It's rather clever if I do say so myself.'

'I've never seen anything like it.'

'I doubt if you have! It's the first of its kind, like the HELOT itself.'

'Why didn't I see it before? I could have helped.'

'I decided not to involve you in its creation. I... I needed to give it my full attention and mine alone. If anything was out of place or damaged in any way... you understand?'

Ludwig nodded reluctantly.

'It's not finished yet, but the final part should be ready soon.' Mandrake returned the device to the drawer and locked it. When he came back he gave his son a look. 'You never answered my question. What do you think?'

'It's incredible.'

His father smiled.

'Good. I'm glad you like it. Now, Mrs Pewsnitt should have our breakfast ready.'

Mandrake clapped his hand on his son's back and led him out of the workshop. As soon as they reached the main hall, they heard the chime of the gates echo through the castle yet again.

'We seem to be in demand these days,' said Mandrake sounding slightly put out. He strolled over to the front door and opened it. 'Ah, Bernard isn't it?"

Ludwig looked around his father and saw a teenage boy standing on the other side with a cap in his hands.

"What can I do for you on this fine morn–' Began Mandrake, but he got no further. The boy in front of him was shaking and his eyes were bright red. 'What is it boy?' Mandrake asked urgently. 'What's happened?'

'I'm sorry, sir,' Bernard began. 'Please, you must come quick!'

Mandrake ran to his study and grabbed two bags, then rushed back into the hall and threw one to Ludwig. As they stepped out the front door, he called for Bernard to lead the way and the trio ran frantically down the track that led from the castle to Little Wainesford.

When they got to the village, Bernard turned and cut though a space between the grocery shop and the blacksmith's, with Mandrake and Ludwig following behind.

The alley opened out onto a broad path that ran between the village and its fields. Bernard stopped and pointed. 'He's in the next field over, sir.'

In the middle of the second field stood a large group of people, all silent and staring. When Bernard, Ludwig and

Mandrake arrived, they pushed their way through with the occasional plea and a gentle hand on a shoulder. The villagers looked up as they passed. They were as white as sheets.

As the trio got closer to the centre, Ludwig saw a woman grab his father's sleeve. 'This is *your* fault!' she hissed. Then one by one, the others started shouting, but his father ignored them.

What's going on? thought Ludwig.

When they reached the middle of the crowd, Ludwig's eyes widened. He turned away, crying out and retching. Now he understood just why the villagers were so angry.

Two years ago, the presentation of the Harvester had been a momentous day in Little Wainesford.

Late one afternoon, Ludwig's father walked along the path that led to his neighbour's farm as the sun set over the trees, turning the sky a soft orange and red. Ludwig was beside him, sitting high up on top of a great metal monstrosity that rolled along with its boiler rumbling and its chimney belching out black smoke.

It was a beast of a machine: eight feet high and twenty or so long, with two great scythes at its front and sleek metal and leather covering the rest of its body. It was like a great, giant beetle but with wheels instead of legs.

Ludwig and his father arrived at the farm as the sun began to disappear. Ludwig let the contraption come to rest in front of the main house, then he dropped to the ground and sat down in the dust. Chickens wandered about around him. His father stood close, wiping the sweat from his forehead.

They waited for a few minutes, but no one came.

Ludwig watched the house and spotted the curtains

twitching in a ground floor window. He glanced at his father, who gave him a knowing smile.

'Mr Arnold?' Mandrake called out. 'Are you there?'

The front door opened and out came the farmer. Mr Arnold took one look at the machine and stopped dead, but seeing Ludwig and his father standing and sitting quite calmly nearby, he plucked up his courage and came closer.

'G-good day Professor. How can I help yer?' he said nervously. His eyes never left the machine for a moment.

'Mr Arnold,' replied Mandrake, 'I think it is *we* who can help *you.*'

'Oh?'

'Both the boy and myself were saddened to hear of the troubles with your crop this year.' Mandrake waved his hands towards the machine. 'Think of this as a gift from one neighbour to another.'

Mr Arnold looked confused and wrung his hands. 'Well, that's very decent of yer sir,' he managed. He peered worryingly at the thing being offered. 'Er... what is it?'

'Allow me to present the Harvester. This machine will let you do your work much faster than normal. No doubt in record time.'

As Mandrake explained what the Harvester could do, Mr Arnold became more interested. He started pacing around the machine, (although each step was a cautious one, as if he was ready to run off should it make any sudden movements towards him). But when Ludwig's father began to tell Mr Arnold how it actually worked, the farmer's face fell.

'So, the driver would sit in the chair, *here,*' explained Mandrake, pointing to the small seat bolted to the front of the machine right above the vicious-looking blades. 'The driver would be strapped in of course...'

'Of course,' said Mr Arnold, letting out a nervous laugh.

'It's perfectly safe,' explained Mandrake. 'Allow me to

demonstrate. Ludwig?'

Ludwig got up off the ground and climbed up onto the Harvester again, using one of the blades as a step. He pulled the straps around himself and locked them in place. Then he started the motor. The Harvester roared into life. Mr Arnold jumped back as Ludwig pushed the brake down, released the wheels, and let the machine rumble forward.

'If you would start the blades,' called out Mandrake when he was a little further away.

Ludwig flicked the switch next to the throttle and the blades below began to churn. Slowly they sped up, occasionally letting out a sharp hiss like paper being torn, but *much* louder.

'Ludwig, now, if you would do as I instructed.'

Ludwig pulled out a small knife from his pocket, opened the blade, and slid it under one of the straps, cutting it cleanly in two. Below him, the blades stopped instantly. The Harvester slowed then stopped, the engine no longer working. Ludwig then waved to his father and the farmer to show he was fine.

'As you can see Mr Arnold, it's perfectly safe,' said Mandrake.

The farmer rubbed his chin. 'It *is* impressive...'

'Obviously if you aren't interested perhaps Mr Nebwell or Mr Delathe might be instead, but I thought I would give you first refusal.'

At the mention of the competition, Mr Arnold suddenly sounded more enthusiastic. 'Oh, no! No need to bother them! Very set in their ways you know, old fashioned. I'm certainly interested. It's a splendid… thing! Splendid!'

The two men shook hands.

'Ludwig!' Mandrake called out when they were done. 'Be so kind as to replace that strap would you? And stay here to show Mr Arnold's driver how to use the Harvester. I will see you at the castle shortly.'

And with a brief nod goodbye, Ludwig watched his father walk off, whistling to himself as he strolled away.

Whilst Ludwig unpacked the tools from the rear of the Harvester, the farmhands began entering the yard from the fields. Mr Arnold called them over as they walked through the gate.

'Listen 'ere!' he called out. 'The Professor and his son have given us a present!'

The farmhands came over, whispering to each other and looking at the machine suspiciously.

'What is it?' shouted one over the murmuring.

Mr Arnold went on to repeat what Ludwig's father had said a short while before. After he finished, he paused, knowing full well what they were going to say next. It came soon enough.

'You want someone to *drive* that?'

'Well... yes,' replied Mr Arnold. 'Perfectly safe ain't it? I watched the boy drive it myself. If the Professor is willing to let his own flesh and blood do it, it must be all right. Stands to reason.' He looked over the unconvinced faces.

'Good luck!' cried someone in the crowd.

'You're mad!' called another.

'Any volunteers?' asked the farmer. 'Anyone?'

Most of the farmhands took one more look at the machine and firmly put their hands behind their backs. A few even began walking away, shaking their heads.

However, near the back of the crowd a solitary hand went up. There was a murmuring and the crowd parted. A man stepped forward.

'I'll do it,' said Mr Pewsnitt.

Back in the field, Ludwig's head swam. It was too horrible. Mr Pewsnitt was in the Harvester and he was badly hurt. Ludwig looked on, dazed, while his father went to Mrs Pewsnitt's husband and rolled up his sleeves.

'He's still alive in there,' someone called out from the crowd. 'You best help 'im or else!'

Ludwig felt his stomach rise. He was going to be sick,

'Ludwig!' cried Mandrake, 'Pass me the tubes and clamps from my bag.' He then knelt down beside the poor man.' We need to tourniquet his legs.'

Ludwig couldn't answer. Instead, he felt his own legs wobble and he crashed to the ground.

Mandrake turned. 'Ludwig pull yourself together! Tubes. Clamps. Now!'

Ludwig groaned, but got his retching under control and shook his head clear. Reaching over to the bag, he pulled out the things and passed them to his father, turning his head carefully as not to catch sight of Mr Pewsnitt again. Then he backed away and sat back down. His father worked frantically, but from what Ludwig had already seen, it didn't look good.

A few minutes later, his father stepped back, shaking his head. 'He's gone,' said Mandrake.

That night, Ludwig woke, terrified. He sat bolt upright and stared out into the darkness, desperate to find a sliver of light and stop the panic. Moonlight shone through a gap between the curtains. He concentrated on it, breathing heavily as the room slowly came into focus.

It had been the third time he had woken up that night. The nightmares came each time he fell asleep. He would see Mr Pewsnitt in the Harvester, groaning in pain and calling out to him while he sat doing nothing; paralysed.

When he had calmed down, he felt for the matches and lit

his lamp. It brightened with a flicker and he let out a sigh of relief. He yawned deeply, but he didn't want to go back to bed. Instead he picked up the lamp, and left his room.

Downstairs, he started to make his way towards the kitchen, but as he crossed the hall he saw light coming out from under the workshop door. When he got closer, he heard odd whining sounds. He pushed the door open and inside, he saw his father standing with his back to him.

'What's going on?' Ludwig called out quietly.

Mandrake span round in surprise and Ludwig cried out. Mr Pewsnitt's blood was still on his clothes.

'My boy. What are you doing up at this hour?'

'I couldn't sleep,' stuttered Ludwig. He tried to look round his father to see what was making that strange noise. 'What are *you* doing?'

'I couldn't sleep either so I thought I'd do some work. And it looks like I've had a flash of inspiration.' Mandrake smiled oddly and moved to one side.

Ludwig gasped and all thoughts of Mr Pewsnitt fled. Behind his father stood the HELOT. The gentle hum and the vibrations in its limbs showed it was working.

'Watch,' said his father, and turned to address the machine. 'HELOT,' he called out. 'Raise your arms.'

The machine appeared to think about this briefly, then raised its arms above its head.

'Lower them,' Mandrake commanded, and again the HELOT did as it was told.

Ludwig's mouth hung open. 'But how? You said you were missing a part?'

'Indeed,' replied his father, 'but as I said, a flash of inspiration struck me.' He walked over to his son and put his arm around his shoulders. 'Would you like to have a go?'

Chapter Four:
Parting

Ludwig and his father stayed in the workshop until the sun came up the following morning. They spent their time teaching the HELOT all kinds of things; it learned so quickly. They started off with simple tasks at first, but after a few hours Ludwig thought they could teach it almost anything. By eleven o'clock, the HELOT was capable of making pots of tea, watering the plants, dusting the surfaces, and all manner of things. Then, later, while Ludwig was trying to teach the machine a magic trick…

'Ludwig, said Mandrake just as the HELOT put a stuffed rabbit into a top hat. 'Because of this development I have to go to Beacon immediately. I need to show this to some people right away. There's no time to lose, I'm afraid. I will be leaving shortly.'

Ludwig turned. 'I thought it was for Mrs Pewsnitt?'

'No, no, I've been thinking it could be used elsewhere, for something more important.'

'But–'

'There's no time to argue. I'm sorry to do this to you but this is too important to delay.'

Ludwig slumped. 'Fine,' he said sullenly.

'Good. I'll go and speak to Mr Shawlworth. I'm sure he will check up on you while I'm away. Mrs Pewsnitt won't be here for obvious reasons, so you will have to make your own meals for a bit I'm afraid.'

Ludwig nodded but didn't want to meet his father's eye.

'I'll be back in a few days. There's enough food in the

pantry and just ask Mr Shawlworth for anything more you need.'

His father turned and was about to walk out when something else occurred to him. 'Oh, one last thing, I won't be around for Mr Pewsnitt's funeral so I would appreciate it if you can go in my place.'

'Me?' said Ludwig, horrified. 'I can't!'

'Please boy, I need your help right now and we must show our faces, despite everything. We owe that to the Pewsnitts at the very least. You know I would not hesitate if there were any other reason...'

Ludwig groaned but nodded his head. 'Okay.'

'Excellent. I promise I'll be back soon.' Mandrake turned and began to hurriedly pack papers into his briefcase before disappearing into the castle.

Ludwig stared at the HELOT as it turned the top hat upside down. The rabbit had disappeared.

The next morning, Ludwig watched his father's carriage trundle down the track with the HELOT strapped to its rear. He waved them goodbye and went back inside.

A couple of days later, Mr Shawlworth came into the castle and found Ludwig in his bedroom. The gardener was dressed in an old suit he wore only for special occasions.

'I said I'd take you lad,' he said.

In the centre of Little Wainesford stood a grey, spired church. Today, its great doors had been flung open and a long line of mourners were walking through the graveyard. When Ludwig and Mr Shawlworth arrived, they joined them and went inside.

Within, Ludwig looked towards the other end of the church and saw Mr Pewsnitt's family in the first few rows. Mrs Pewsnitt was there, holding a handkerchief and dabbing her eyes occasionally. Next to her were her children, all looking as sad as their mother. Behind the Pewsnitts were the farmhands and Mr Arnold. Most of them had been there when the accident happened. Last of all was the rest of the village. Ludwig and Mr Shawlworth sat at the back.

A few feet away from the front row was a simple, wooden coffin. Ludwig felt a lump in his throat when he saw it. He turned his eyes away and caught sight of the villagers looking at him. Their eyes were hard and piercing. He shuffled closer to the gardener and hid his face in the old man's arm.

'Ignore 'em lad,' said Mr Shawlworth quietly in Ludwig's ear. 'They jus' don't understand. It weren't your fault, nor your father's.'

Ludwig swallowed and nodded. At the front, he heard a raised voice from near the altar. He looked up and saw Father Wentworth beginning the ceremony.

The priest spoke of Mr Pewsnitt being a good father, a caring husband and a generous friend, and every word was torture for Ludwig. After he had finished, a few hymns were sung. Finally the priest nodded and Mr Pewsnitt's sons stood and took their places around the coffin. Father Wentworth stepped in front of them and the sons followed behind with their father on their shoulders. As they passed each pew, those seated rose and followed them outside until the entire congregation had left the building.

A short while later, Mr Pewsnitt was committed to the ground and the mourners started making their way out of the graveyard. Father Wentworth and Mrs Pewsnitt stood nearby, thanking everyone who had come. Ludwig and Mr Shawlworth stood in line.

'I'm sorry father isn't here,' said Ludwig when he reached

them. 'Something important came up and he had to go to Beacon. He–' but before he could finish, Mrs Pewsnitt bent down and hugged him tightly.

'Don't worry love,' she whispered into his ear. 'I got a letter from him earlier. He sends his best. But thank *you* for coming. It means a lot.'

She held on to Ludwig for a long time, until eventually he had to look to Mr Shawlworth for help. The gardener let out a little cough and touched Mrs Pewsnitt's arm lightly. She let go of Ludwig and took Mr Shawlworth in her arms instead.

'I'm Sorry, Dot,' said the gardener. 'If there's anything I can do...'

'Oh, Arthur,' she replied, hugging the man hard. Finally she let both of them go on their way and others took their place in her embrace.

'I'm going over to the Lantern and Parapet to see everyone,' said Mr Shawlworth when they reached the Lychgate. 'Do you want to come along?'

Ludwig shook his head. He didn't want to see those accusing faces again.

Mr Shawlworth looked at Ludwig sadly and patted him on the shoulder. 'Don't worry lad, they'll be fine in a day or two. I'll have a word. Accidents happen.' He stepped into the road. 'Can you make it back to the castle on your own?'

Ludwig nodded and watched Mr Shawlworth walk off towards the other villagers. He turned, and was about to set off home when he saw Mrs Pewsnitt sitting on a bench next to her husband's grave, all alone. Ludwig hesitated at first, wondering if he should disturb her, then began to make his way over to the bench, treading softly as if not to upset those lying underneath his feet.

'Mrs Pewsnitt?' he called out when he was closer.

The housekeeper lifted her head and looked at him. Her eyes were red but at the sight of Ludwig she gave a smile.

'I'm so sorry!' Ludwig blurted out. 'We never meant—' but before he could continue, she rose and took his hand.

'It weren't your fault, dear,' she said quietly. She put her arm around Ludwig and pulled him down to the church bench.

Ludwig sobbed.

'Come on love. Don't be like that.'

He tried to reply but he couldn't. Nothing would come.

'These things happen,' said the housekeeper. 'You and your father were only trying to help. I've known yer all your life and I know you haven't got a wicked bone in yer body.'

Ludwig wiped his eyes with his cuff and Mrs Pewsnitt gave him a squeeze.

'He liked you a lot, did you know that? And your father too. You were the reason he volunteered to drive yer contraption in the first place. He trusted you. He knew you would never do anythin' that put anyone in danger.'

'The others don't think so.'

'They'll come round. They're angry that's all, and they don't know you and your father like I do. They're only lookin' for someone to blame.'

'Maybe...'

'Course, love,' said Mrs Pewsnitt, sitting back. She reached out and picked one of the small, blue flowers that grew on the graveyard wall. She lifted it to her nose and sniffed. 'I've missed you, you know that? Arranging the funeral and bein' with my family, I've missed being up there with you two, an' Arthur of course. I hope you're surviving without me...' She gave Ludwig a little smile.

'Just about, Mrs Pewsnitt,' Ludwig replied.

'By the by, did you have a good time with Sir Notsworth, dear? Oh, he's a character and no mistake.'

Notsworth? Thought Ludwig. It felt like years had passed since Ludwig had seen him, but it had only been a few days.

'I– I found out about my brother.'

'Oh good dear, that *is* a relief.'

Ludwig stared at the housekeeper in surprise. Her eyes were closed as she sniffed her flower. She didn't see his face.

'Did your father finally tell you?'

'Not exactly,' Ludwig stuttered. 'I overheard Notsworth and father talking.'

'Well, at least you know now. I've been wondering how long it would take.'

'You knew?' He tried to keep his voice sounding normal.

'Of course dear.' She let out a sad little laugh. 'I felt ever so guilty not telling yer, but your father was very clear on the matter. I've always thought it was unfair, but I suppose he had his reasons. So, what do you think of him?'

'What do I think of him?'

'Don't be like that. He may be a bit odd. But he's lovely once you get to know him.'

'*You've met him?*'

She pushed the flower into a button hole and opened her eyes. 'Who do you think looks after him?'

'Well...' Ludwig began.

'I do, that's who. It's a pleasure though. He's a real gent.'

'Can you tell me about... er...' *What did Notsworth call him?* 'Hephaestus?'

'Why don't you ask him yourself?'

'I would, but... but I haven't met him yet.'

'I understand dear. It's a hard thing to get used to with him being so different. But I feel so bad seeing him all alone in the cellars. Your father does his best but–, Ludwig?'

She looked up and saw Ludwig running back to the castle as fast as his legs could carry him.

'You're right,' she said to her husband's grave. 'He *is* a strange boy.'

Chapter Five: Hephaestus

Ludwig shot through the great hall and the kitchens towards the cellar entrance at the far end of the long gallery. When he got to the the door, he opened it and stopped dead. Beyond, it was *pitch* black.

It's just the cellars, Ludwig told himself, but his imagination was getting the better of him. He thought about running back to the kitchen to grab a knife, just in case, but if his brother was down there, showing up with a weapon might not be such a good idea.

Behind him, the lanterns hanging on the walls had lit themselves as evening had set in. Ludwig took one and turned the dial to make the flame brighter. That would have to do.

He returned to the door and began making his way downwards, walking slowly as the light uncovered the steps in front of him. His heart pounded. It was one of the most terrifying things he had ever done.

At the bottom, the stairwell opened up into a musty room full of columns holding up low arches. Ludwig saw racks full of dusty wine bottles all along the walls. When he looked at the floor he saw footprints. It occurred to him that Mrs Pewsnitt must come down here every day for the wine his father drank, and here he was, scared to death!

He carried on, passing through more vaults filled with rubbish and old inventions that had never worked, whose shadows got his imagination going in ways he never wanted. Finally he came to a vault that was bare except for a simple wood door built into one of its walls.

He took a deep breath and knocked.

And waited...

And waited some more...

... And nothing happened.

Feeling slightly put out, Ludwig pressed his ear to the woodwork and listened carefully. There was no sound on the other side. He huffed irritably, then slowly reached out and turned the iron handle. It was unlocked. Pushing the door open, Ludwig suddenly threw his arms across his eyes as blinding light flooded out of the room. He waited a few moments until he thought he was ready and looked again... and gasped.

In the next room, he saw books and papers *everywhere*. They were piled against each wall and scattered across the floor, lit up by an old iron chandelier hanging from the ceiling. He walked over to one heap and picked up the first book he came to. *Lead into Gold: the Alchemist's Conundrum* by Calvinius Gaia. Then he picked up another: *Theories of Light* by Ignacious P. Farnhertz. Ludwig recognised them all. It was like someone had taken the books from his father's library, put them in a great stack and blew them up. This room was the result.

At the other end of the room was another door. Ludwig walked over and pressed his ear to it. This time he could hear something on the other side. He took another deep breath and knocked.

'What is it?' boomed a voice that was so deep it was felt more than heard.

Ludwig, rigid with fright, couldn't reply.

'Mrs Pewsnitt? Is that you?'

Ludwig was about to turn and run when the door opened.

Standing in the doorway was a terrible sight. It was human shaped but well over seven feet tall, with massive arms and hands that nearly touched the floor. On top of its chest was a short neck, and on top of that was a horrific face. Its mouth gaped open with teeth at all angles like they had been hit with a hammer. Its nose was small and turned up pig-like. Small eyes peered out under bushy brows. The creature reached down and picked Ludwig up by the back of his shirt, lifting him up and bringing him face to terrible face.

Ludwig closed his eyes and hoped whatever happened next wouldn't hurt.

'Ludwig?' the creature rumbled.

Ludwig opened one eye.

'Hephaestus?'

Something that might have been a smile spread across the monster's face.

'This is amazing!' cried Ludwig as he was put down.

'It's very strange certainly,' said the creature, watching as Ludwig darted around him excitedly.

'I can't believe you're here. All this time and I've never known!'

'You weren't meant to know,' said Hephaestus, not unkindly. He sat down on a huge bed that stretched across the back wall. It creaked under the weight. 'How did you find out about me?'

Ludwig looked both sad and ashamed. He told his brother about Mr Pewsnitt's accident and Mrs Pewsnitt in the graveyard, and what he had heard between his father and Notsworth.

'Mr Pewsnitt's dead? That's terrible. Father never said anything. He just said Mrs Pewsnitt would be away for a while.'

'I feel awful,' Laudwig said.

'Mrs Pewsnitt is right. It wasn't your fault.'

Ludwig didn't want to talk about it. Instead, he looked around his brother's room and saw paintings covering most of the walls. He went over to get a better look at them. 'You did these?' he asked.

'It's a hobby.'

'They're really good.'

He peered at one that showed a bizarre sea creature. It looked like it was actually moving. He lent closer.

'Take one if you like.'

'Really? Thanks!' Ludwig shifted and stared at his feet, then went to the bed and sat down. 'I wish father hadn't needed to lie about you,' he said quietly.

'He cares too much, that's all. I think he was worried you wouldn't cope–' the creature swung his hands around his face and body '– with this.'

'He didn't need to be.'

Hephaestus grinned.

Chapter Six:
All Change

'I think we should we go upstairs,' said Ludwig a few days later. 'You should see the rest of the castle. And we can surprise father when he gets back. We can be like a proper family.'

The brothers had spent all their time together since they had found each other. They told each other about their lives, and Ludwig told Hephaestus stories about the people in the village. But they had been in the cellars all that while and, quite frankly, Ludwig was getting sick of it.

'I don't think I can go,' said Hephaestus. He stood against the far wall looking fearfully at the door. 'If anyone saw, and so soon after what happened to Mr Pewsnitt, they could turn on father…'

'It'll be okay. Come on, no one will know.' Ludwig went to the door and held it open.

Hephaestus shuffled forward and peered into the darkness. 'No...'

Ludwig took one of his brother's great hands. 'Just follow me,' he said, tugging on Hephaestus gently.

'Well...,' said Hephaestus and he slowly took a step forward.

'That's it,' said Ludwig. 'That's it.'

Soon both brothers were walking through the cellars.

'Where are we going?' asked Hephaestus nervously.

'Anywhere you like,' replied Ludwig. 'When father finds out I know about you, he'll let you live upstairs I'm sure. We can all help to hide you. Mrs Pewsnitt knows about you anyway and Mr Shawlworth's very nice.'

When they got to the long gallery, sunlight was shining through the windows.

Hephaestus covered his eyes. 'I don't remember the sun being so bright…'

'Wait here,' said Ludwig. 'I need to make sure it's safe. Just in case.' He ran on through the kitchens and out into the gardens where Mr Shawlworth was planting flowers in the hole the cannon had made.

'Hello lad!' the gardener called out when he saw Ludwig.

'I'm going to be studying in the library today,' said Ludwig quickly. 'So don't worry about checking up on me.'

The old gardener looked at him and shrugged. 'Right you are. Just give me a shout if you need anything.'

'Sure,' replied Ludwig, running back to the castle. Inside, he found Hephaestus staring curiously at paintings of von Guggenstein's past that hung on the walls of the long gallery.

'Let's go,' said Ludwig. Hephaestus nodded and the two of them walked through the castle, Ludwig leading his brother to the library. 'Mr Shawlworth won't come in here if he knows I'm working,' explained Ludwig.

Hephaestus nodded and stepped through the library's door. 'Interesting,' he said when they were inside. He pulled a book out of one of the shelves and flicked through its pages, 'I've read so many of these...' Then he walked over to the piano, lifted the cover, and touched a few keys.

'Can you play?' asked Ludwig.

'No. I'm not allowed any instruments. The noise...' Hephaestus shrugged and looked over to his brother. 'What shall we do now?'

Ludwig ran over to the desk at the far end of the library. 'Well,' he said, pulling out paper and pencils. 'I thought you could teach me to draw like you.' He took the piano stool and armchair and put them on the other side of the desk so they would be looking out of the window and over the fields and forests around the castle.

'It took me years to learn!' said Hephaestus.

'Are we in a rush?' Ludwig replied.

The next evening, as Hephaestus continued with his lessons, the brothers heard the main doors of the castle bang closed. They both looked up.

'Wait here,' said Ludwig. He left the library and went downstairs. When he reached the main hall, he caught sight of his father going into the workshop.

'Those blasted fools!' Ludwig heard his father mutter to himself. 'How dare they!'

In the workshop, Ludwig found his father pacing the floor, looking very annoyed.

'How *dare* they! Peace! Bah, surrender more like!'

Ludwig stood in the doorway and coughed to get his father's attention.

'But what can be done?' continued Mandrake. 'That's the question! Maybe–'

'Father?'

Mandrake looked up, startled. 'Ludwig? My boy, it's good to see you! Oh, you don't know what a time I've had. Weeks wasted trying to convince those…those idiots to–' he glanced at the HELOT. 'It doesn't matter,' he sighed. The anger seemed to drain from his voice and he looked tired. 'How have you been? The funeral… was it bearable?'

'I suppose so. But a few people gave me bad looks.'

'I was worried about that. We may get them for a while.'

'And…I learned something.'

Mandrake looked at his son. 'You *have* been busy.'

'From Mrs Pewsnitt.'

'Really? If you've been bothering her...'

'I want to show you something.'

Ludwig took his father's hand and led him out of the workshop. Mandrake looked at him puzzled and the HELOT followed dutifully behind.

'Ludwig, where are we going?' asked his father as they walked up the stairs. 'I have lots of work to do. I'm sorry, but I don't have time for your games right now. I have plans...'

'Please, you'll see in a minute. I think you'll like it.' Ludwig pushed open the library doors and walked through. 'It's okay,' he continued. 'You don't have to lie to me any more.' He pointed over to the desk where his brother was sitting.

'Hephaestus?' cried Mandrake.

Ludwig ran over and stood next to his brother. 'I found him, father, and we get on, we really do! I know you were afraid I would be scared or upset, but I'm not!'

Mandrake looked furious. 'Ludwig, that's not–' But before he could continue, Hephaestus jumped up as the HELOT came into view.

'Don't worry,' said Ludwig. 'It's just the HELOT. It can even do magic tricks! I taught it–'

'It's an abomination!' Hephaestus cried. He bounded towards the machine, but stopped in his tracks when his father raised a hand and pressed it to his chest.

'Don't be stupid boy. Leave it alone.'

Ludwig watched confused as Hephaestus looked down at his father and leaned close. He whispered something that Ludwig couldn't hear and his father's eye's flashed to Ludwig.

'Watch your tongue!' Mandrake hissed.

Hephaestus turned and looked at his brother horrified. 'Did Ludwig *help* you? No...'

'Ludwig doesn't know the details,' replied Mandrake. 'But yes, he helped. He's proud to have done so.'

'What's going on?' Ludwig asked.

'It's not important,' replied Mandrake. 'I'm very angry with you by the way, young man.'

'You're angry with *him*!' cried Hephaestus. 'You... you monster!'

Ludwig looked up and saw his brother raising a great fist over the machine. 'No!' he cried out, running over. 'You can't!'

Hephaestus brought his fist down and looked hard at his brother. 'You don't understand...'

'Silence!' Screamed Mandrake.

'He should know!' said Hephaestus.

'HELOT!' cried Mandrake, pointing at Hephaestus. 'Take him back to the cellars.'

Ludwig watched in horror as the machine launched itself at Hephaestus without even pausing.

Hephaestus crashed to the ground with the machine on top of him. He tried to push it away but it dug its feet into the floor and its hands pressed him down. The HELOT was small compared to him, but it was strong.

'Stop!' Ludwig cried out as the HELOT seized his brother's feet and start dragging him outside.

Hephaestus bellowed and reached out for anything that could hold him back. Bookshelves came tumbling down as he grabbed for them, but the pull of the machine was too great.

'Ludwig you stupid, *stupid* boy,' said his father, ignoring what was happening. 'I am *so* disappointed in you.'

Ludwig looked at his father and his mouth fell open.

Mandrake grabbed him and pulled him out of the

library. 'You will stay in your room until I'm ready to deal with you.'

While he was dragged along the landing, Ludwig could hear his brother roaring and yelling as the HELOT took him away. When they got to his bedroom, his father threw him inside and then slammed the door shut. Ludwig fell on the floor with tears in his eyes and behind him, there was a click as the door was locked. He didn't even know there was a key.

This can't be happening...

He got up, ran to the door and pressed his ear to it, but there was no sound. He tried to open it, but it wouldn't budge. Finally, he beat on the door with his fists. Nothing happened. Suddenly, Ludwig remembered the grate. He got up and ran over to the drawers, pulling them away from the wall and dropping onto his stomach to listen. It was very quiet, but he could faintly hear something in his father's study.

'...Should have done this a long time ago...' came his father's voice. 'Such a shame... such a shame... too dangerous...' A drawer banged open. 'This ends now... where's that *blasted* pistol...'

No!

Ludwig jumped up, ran over to the window and pushed it open. Looking out, he saw the long drop to the ground, but to one side old, green creepers covered the castle walls. He had wanted to climb them for years but never dared.

Steeling himself, he reaching out, grabbed a vine and pulled himself outside. Each movement was sheer terror. The vines creaked and sometimes gave way, but slowly, ever so slowly, he made his way down.

When he got the bottom, he jumped off and ran to the door to the kitchens. He pushed it open slightly and took a look around. There was no sign of his father. He opened the door some more and crept through, careful not to make a sound. Soon enough, he got to the long gallery. At the end, he could see the cellar door was open. He ran in and dived down into the darkness yet again.

Below, Ludwig walked as quietly as he could, staying near the walls and trying not to think about whatever might be lurking there with him. After what seemed like an eternity, and barely daring to breathe, he got to the last cellar and froze.

The HELOT was standing outside Hephaestus' door.

Its motors whined as Ludwig crept closer, but with each step he took the machine did nothing. Ludwig didn't even blink fearing the HELOT was about to jump at him any second, but even when he stood right next to it, it remained still. Ludwig sighed with relief and pressed on.

He opened the first door to his brother's rooms slowly. Inside, all the books that had been scattered around had been pushed to one side and a trail led down the middle. In the next room, Ludwig could hear his father.

'Hephaestus,' said Mandrake, 'I'm sorry, but I can't have you corrupting Ludwig, not now. He's too young and too important, and if anyone else found out... you understand.'

'Corrupt? You monster!' Hephaestus bellowed. 'You *monster*!'

'Goodbye Hephaestus. You have done so much for me. I *am* sorry.'

Ludwig ran at the door. It burst open and his father turned around in surprise as Ludwig jumped into the air and landed on his back. 'No!' Ludwig shouted. 'Leave him alone!'

'What are you-?' shouted Mandrake, trying to grab hold of his son. 'Get off me, boy!'

'I won't let you hurt him!'

'Enough! HELOT! Help me! Ludwig, for Azmon's sake– No!'

Then, for Ludwig, the world went black.

Chapter Seven: Escape!

Hephaestus burst through the front door of the castle. Splintered wood and iron hinges flew across the courtyard as it collapsed around him. While he ran, he looked down. Ludwig was in his arms. He held his brother tight, not sure whether he was dead or alive. His free hand was laid against Ludwig's head where a long cut was bleeding badly.

When Hephaestus reached the village, he stopped and looked back. Staring into the darkness, he waited until he was sure they weren't being followed. Then, out of the corner of his eye, he caught sight of a water pump lit by the nearby building. He walked over to it, treading cautiously.

Suddenly Ludwig moved his hand.

He's alive!

Hephaestus took the pump's handle and pushed down. When the trough had filled a little, he scooped up some water and held it to his brother's mouth. He watched as it made Ludwig stir. When Ludwig was finished, Hephaestus tenderly placed his damp hand on his brother's forehead and tried to clean away some of the blood.

'I'm so sorry,' he whispered quietly. 'I'm so sorry.'

Unfortunately, it was at this moment that Mr Barnhill and Mr Fallowstaff decided to leave the Lantern and Parapet. They came out, but stopped dead in their tracks when they saw Hephaestus with Ludwig in his arms. Too shocked to say or do anything, they stared wide-eyed at the strange sight, their voices trapped in their throats. However, they were soon brought to their senses when Ludwig groaned loudly and twisted in his brother's hands.

'Wait–' Hephaestus began, but got no further. The two men turned and ran back inside the pub. Through the doorway, he could hear shouting and chairs hitting the floor. Not waiting for them return, Hephaestus threw Ludwig over his shoulder and ran.

Through the village and into the fields he went, smashing fences and jumping walls. Behind him, Hephaestus could hear the villagers' cries and he couldn't help but imagine the murderous things they must be saying. He ran on and soon got to the far woods just as the villagers had reached the fields. Then he heard the barking of dogs.

Moving frantically now through the woods and hoping above all else the dogs were on leashes, Hephaestus spied a group of larger trees whose low branches looked thick and sturdy. He put his brother down and looked at him.

'Ludwig, I need you hold on to me. We need to hide.'

Ludwig reached out without even looking and put his arms around his brother's neck. Hephaestus swung him around so he rested against his back and waited for his brother to grasp his waist with his legs.

'Hold on tight,' said Hephaestus, taking hold of the first branch. Behind him, he could hear the villagers getting closer and the dogs' barks getting louder. He pulled on the branch and began hauling them upwards towards the possible safety of the tree-tops. Higher and higher they went until the branches looked strong enough for both of them to sit on without falling. When they were as high as they could go, Hephaestus put his brother down and waited. Below them, he could hear the villagers crashing through the woods.

'Anyone found 'em?' cried out Mr Barnhill as he stumbled into the clearing.

When the others emerged out of the trees, each one shook their heads. They stopped near Mr Barnhill and began milling about in the clearing, staring into the night and wishing their lanterns could be brighter.

'Did anyone recognise the boy?' asked Father Wentworth. The priest had seen the villagers run by his cottage and the shouts of "demon" had stirred his curiosity enough to venture outside. If there was a demon, he didn't want to miss it.

'You know, I could've sworn it were the Professor's lad,' said Mr Fallowstaff.

'Oh!' said Father Wentworth. 'And after all that happened with Mr Pewsnitt...'

'Skinny lad ain't he? Young 'un?'

A few of the others nodded.

'Bet the Professor's let loose some monster!' said Mr Barnhill.

'Wouldn't put it past him,' said Mr Arnold. 'Odd things go on up there at that castle of his, I'm sure of it.'

There was a murmuring of agreement and the others looked around nervously. They huddled together and realised there weren't that many of them after all. Then, with make-shift weapons in hand, they went off in the direction of Castle Guggenstein.

Hephaestus watched the villagers go and breathed out in relief. When he was sure they were far enough away, he picked up his brother, climbed down the tree, and ran into the darkness of the woods and away from Little Wainesford.

Chapter Eight:
The Future is Unwritten

The next morning, Ludwig woke and cried out as the ground rushed up to meet him. He would have hit it too if it wasn't for Hephaestus and his quick hands. 'We're in a tree?' he asked, sitting back on the branch. He looked around and saw treetops all around him. Birds squawked as they flew past.

'Seemed like the safest place,' shrugged Hephaestus, yawning.

As Ludwig's eyes wandered, the pain hit him. 'Oh, my head!' he cried, pressing his hand to the cut on the forehead. It felt sticky and when he took his hand away, he saw blood. 'What *happened*?'

'What do you remember?' asked Hephaestus as he tore a piece of his shirt into a strip and began patching up Ludwig's wound.

'I remember father seeing you– Ouch!'

'Hold still.'

'That hurt! … You were angry about the HELOT. You went to hit it and father made it take you away.' Ludwig groaned. 'He was going to kill you!'

'And you came to rescue me,' said Hephaestus. 'When you jumped on father, the HELOT tried to protect him. It pulled you off and you hit your head. I thought...I thought it had killed you. It went after you again, but I knocked it back and it crashed into father. They were both on the floor when I left. I ran out of the castle with you over my shoulder, but then the villagers saw me and chased me away. We've been in the woods ever since. I didn't know what else to do.'

'Is father still alive?'

'I think so. The HELOT fell on him, but I heard him shouting as I ran.'

Ludwig paused. 'What do we do now?'

'I can't go back.'

'But–' began Ludwig, but he went silent when he saw his brother's face.

'Everything's gone wrong, Ludwig, I can't return, not now. You heard what father wanted to do to me. I'm not safe there anymore. And the villagers saw me too. After what happened with Mr Pewsnitt, I wouldn't even get a chance to explain.' Hephaestus let out a gruff, sad laugh. 'It's strange. I had a feeling something was going to go wrong some time. Never thought it would be like this though.'

Ludwig was about to argue but he knew his brother was right. Their father had tried to kill him, and now all of Little Wainesford knew that a monster was roaming the area. What else could he do? 'So where will we go?' asked Ludwig.

Hephaestus looked up surprised. '"We"?'

'I'm coming with you.'

'You don't have to do that, Ludwig. Go back. I'll be okay. Just be careful. I think… I think father is doing things he shouldn't.'

'Like the HELOT?'

Hephaestus nodded.

Ludwig touched the bandage on his head. Then he thought about the lock on his door and his father's face when he saw him with Hephaestus. He remembered listening to his father getting ready to kill; it was like he was doing something so ordinary, as if Hephaestus wasn't his son, just something that needed to be dealt with. 'I don't want to go back,' Ludwig said finally. The words felt unnatural but right all the same. 'I don't think I can.'

Chapter Nine:
A New Life

On the sixth morning, Ludwig was woken by something cold against his cheek. He brushed it away and rolled over on the dry ground to get some more sleep.

They'd been travelling for *so* long now and Ludwig could barely remember what a bed even felt like. The days had passed and they walked and walked and walked, avoiding anywhere where there might be people. They lived off berries and roots and slept on piles of leaves and moss. It was horrible, and right now no animal was going to wake him out of curiosity.

The cold thing touched him again. It jabbed him hard.

'Go away!' mumbled Ludwig.

'Get up, boy. Now.'

Ludwig's eyes shot open. That was no animal. He turned and saw a man standing over him with a pistol in his hand. It was pointed right at him. Ludwig scrambled across the ground, desperate to get away, but the man watched him and laughed cruelly.

'Where do you think you're goin'? said the man. He walked over to Ludwig, grabbed him by his shirt, then lifted him up and threw him back down into the dirt. He smiled as Ludwig yelped in pain. Then he tucked his pistol in his belt and pulled out a vicious-looking knife. 'Perhaps I need to clip yer wings a bit, as it were,' he said, bending down; but as he reached out to Ludwig, a voice came over his shoulder.

'Don't you hurt 'im, Jack. They're no use to us dead.'

The man looked back. 'Aye, Captain, I know. I was just makin' sure he doesn't go running off. He'll heal.'

The man lent down again and his blade touched Ludwig's skin.

Ludwig squeezed his eyes shut.

'Jack! What's wrong with yer?' came the voice. 'Leave 'im alone!'

The man grunted in irritation and looked at Ludwig as if it was his fault he was going to miss out on his fun. He sheathed his knife, picked Ludwig up, and dropped him on his feet.

'Later, boy,' he whispered.

Ludwig looked up and saw two more men in front of him, both with pistols in their hands. Next to them sat Hephaestus. He was tied with strong-looking ropes and was staring miserably at the ground. He caught Ludwig's eye when Ludwig came closer, but turned his head away quickly.

'Captain,' said one of the men, nudging his gun against Hephaestus. 'We've got a right brute here. He'll do perfect.'

'Aye, mate,' said the other who had been called "Captain". 'He certainly will.'

The Captain looked over to Ludwig and his eyes narrowed. Across his face, Ludwig could see strange patterns; swirling shapes that covered his cheeks and forehead and carried on down his neck. His hair was dark, curly and short, and he had rings all along the edge of one ear. He looked like no one Ludwig had ever seen before. When the Captain saw Ludwig staring at him, he gave him a big grin, full of perfect, white teeth.

'What d'you want with this one?' grunted the man who had woken Ludwig, prodding his captive hard in the shoulder. 'Can't see us needing *him*. You sure you don't want me to–'

Ludwig heard the knife being drawn again.

Leave 'im Jack. He's comin' with us,' said the Captain, sharply. 'We could do with an extra hand around the place anyhow. Load 'em in the carriage. I'll give them a quick talking to and tell them what's what.'

The man laughed and picked Ludwig up, slinging him over his shoulder. Ludwig struggled, but the man cuffed him around the head whenever he tried to wriggle free. He soon gave up. 'You're learning, boy,' said the man called Jack.

Then they began walking. Ten minutes later they stopped again.

'Throw 'em inside,' came the voice of the Captain.

There was a pause, and seconds later the world blurred. Ludwig was taken off Jack's shoulder and pushed up some steps backwards. He fell onto a floor and dazed, caught sight of a door closing.

'You. Help him up,' came the voice of the Captain.
Ludwig felt himself being lifted and dropped on a bench. He squinted in the darkness and could just about make out Hephaestus sitting next to him.

The Captain was opposite. He lent forward to cut Hephaestus' bonds, and then did the same for Ludwig. 'Now–'

'We're not going back!' Ludwig cried out suddenly.

'Good for you,' replied the Captain.

'We're *not!* You can't make us!'

'The shoutin' is useful. Keep it up. They need to hear that outside.'

'What–' but before Ludwig could carry on, he felt his brother's hand on his arm.

'I don't think father sent him.'

Ludwig looked at the Captain suspiciously. 'Why?'

'I wouldn't be alive for a start.'

The Captain laughed. 'Aye, you're a bright one!' he nodded to Hephaestus then looked at Ludwig. 'No lad, the gentleman here is correct. I don't work for yer father. I *do* know him though.'

'How?' asked Hephaestus and Ludwig together.

The Captain laughed again. 'Like I'm goin' to tell yer straight out! No lad, best if we kept that quiet for now, for your sake as much as anythin'.' He peered at Ludwig. 'I know about you too, lad. It's Ludwig isn't it? Ha, by that look, I know I'm right.' He then looked at Hephaestus. 'But *you* I don't know. You came as a bit of a surprise if you don't mind me sayin', although you were a godsend. All this way just for an ordinary looking lad would have raised questions, but you...'

'Don't tell him anything,' said Ludwig.

'I think he knows enough already,' replied Hephaestus. 'I'm Hephaestus, Ludwig's brother.'

The Captain looked surprised. 'You're brothers? Really? Well, that is interestin'. Your father's got more secrets than even I guessed.' He stared at Hephaestus for a few seconds, rubbing his chin.

'What do you want with us?' asked Ludwig.

'I heard about yer disappearance, so I came to pick you up before yer father got you. Although *I* heard a monster had kidnapped you. Instead, I find yer've got a brother and are on the run instead! Will wonders ever cease! But that's all by the by and we ain't got time to chat right now. Just remember that I'm 'ere to help.' The Captain jerked his thumb at the carriage wall. 'I should go. They'll be wondering what I'm doing with you if I take any longer.' He lent over to the door and was about to open it when Ludwig spoke again.

'We don't need your help.'

The Captain sat back down and looked at Ludwig. 'Really? What were yer goin' to do instead? Wander the woods the rest of yer lives? You can't go to any towns or cities. If you managed not to get chased out or worse, your father would hear about yer soon enough. He's got eyes *everywhere* that one. And you ain't got much choice right now. You can take yer chances with me, or... well...'

Ludwig heard the click of the Captain's pistol.

'You wouldn't!'

'Don't push me, lad. You're swimmin' with sharks. It ain't your fault, but that's they way it is.'

Ludwig was about to say something, but stopped when he heard his brother.

'It looks like we don't have a choice,' said Hephaestus.

'Now yer thinkin',' replied the Captain, grinning again. 'With me looking after yer, you've nothing to fear.'

The brothers caught each other's eye but said nothing as the Captain left.

It was dark and hot inside the carriage as it bumped along to wherever the brothers were being taken. The only light came from cracks and holes in the carriage's walls and ceiling. They could just about make out each other, but little else.

'We need to escape,' said Ludwig when he was sure the noise of the carriage's wheels would cover their voices.

'I'm not so sure,' rumbled Hephaestus, staring at the side of the carriage where a window should have been. 'I think we'll be safe enough for the time being.'

'He threatened to kill us!'

'He only threatened. I don't think he wants us dead. And he lied to his own men, you heard that yourself. He's putting himself in danger for us so we must be important enough to keep alive. I think we can trust him, but I don't know why.'

'The pistol...' said Ludwig quietly.

'He wouldn't have used it.'

'Are you sure?

Hephaestus didn't reply.

Some time later, the carriage came to a halt and the door swung open. The man called Jack was on the other side, his pistol drawn. 'Out you come, gents. We're here, as it were.'

The brothers stepped outside. They looked to the horizon and saw the sun was already going down. They must have been traveling for the entire day.

'Move,' growled Jack impatiently.

They followed the Captain and the other men as they disappeared around the side of the carriage. On the other side, they came to quite a sight. In front of them, standing in the middle of the field, was a huge, striped tent, surrounded by other smaller, brightly coloured tents and decorated carriages. People were milling about between them, chatting to each other and carrying things from one place to another. Occasionally there was the roar of animals.

The Captain stopped and turned to the brothers. 'Welcome to yer new home mates, for the time bein' at least. This way if yer please.'

The brothers followed him through the tents and carriages to an area behind the big top. Jack pushed them whenever they slowed to look at the sights. Of all the places they imagined they'd find at the end of their journey, this wasn't one of them.

The Captain led the brothers to a smaller tent and ushered them inside. He dismissed Jack, who slunk off to join some other men nearby, and then sat down behind a battered old desk and put his boots up. He lent back, making his chair creak, and looked the brothers over.

'Right, first things first. This is *my* circus, and you're going to be working for *me*. Got that? I don't know how long you'll be here but I want you kept safe, and for now this is the best place. Yer just two strays, no one will think different. Besides, everyone here is hidin' or runnin' from something, so no one will ask questions. Some of the boys were a bit rough with yer when we picked you up, but don't hold a grudge, they were under orders to scare yer. It's the way we do things. You might get a little trouble from some of 'em, everyone does, but it's nothing serious. Just look worried for the next few days until you've got used to things and no one will raise an eyebrow.'

The brothers listened dumbstruck.

'I know yer confused and scared,' the Captain went on. 'But this is for the best.'

When he finished, the tent flaps opened and a smartly dressed man stepped in. He was clean and neat, with a thin, dark mustache that curled at the ends. He looked very different from the others the brothers had seen so far in the circus. 'Hello Captain,' he said.

'Boys, this is Dr Angelus. He's what I like to call my first mate. Dr Angelus, this is "*Lian*" and "*Hector*".'

The new man nodded to the brothers.

'Dr Angelus is going to be looking after yer from day to day. If you got any problems, go to him. Understand?'

Then Ludwig and Hephaestus managed a nod.

'Good. Doctor, put that one...' The Captain looked at Ludwig, '... with Gill. He should be in the galley. Put the other one with Terantless. He'd appreciate a new entertainer.'

Dr Angelus nodded and turned to the brothers. 'Come with me please gentlemen.'

As the man called Dr Angelus walked out of the tent, Ludwig turned to the Captain, his voice finally coming to him. 'Then what?' he demanded. 'What's going to happen to us?'

'I've told yer. You'll be safe. That's better than your previous situation. Trust me. All I can tell you is that yer father is very dangerous, and its best you weren't near him.

Now go with Dr Angelus, he'll see yer right.'

The Captain picked up a paper on the desk and started reading. 'Go on now,' he said without looking up.

'So, gentlemen,' began Dr Angelus as they walked through the circus. 'I think you will be happy enough here. Lian, you'll be with Gill. I think you will find him fair.'
They came to an area full of large, plain tents tucked away from the rest of the circus. Dr Angelus led the brothers up to one of the biggest and pulled aside a flap. Inside were rows of tables and benches, and at one end a man and a woman were cooking in huge pots. Rich smells drifted through the air, reminding the brothers they hadn't eaten hot food in a long time.

'This is the galley where you will come for your meals. Gill and Terantless will show you where your bunks are. Fortunately, we've managed to get you quarters to share just between the two of you.' Dr Angelus led the boys to one table where a small group of men were finishing their dinners. 'Gill?' said the Doctor.

One of the men at the table stood up and nodded to Dr Angelus. Down across one eye was a long scar and another smaller one cut across the other cheek touching his mouth. He looked mean. 'Aye sir?'

'This one,' Dr Angelus pushed Ludwig forward, 'is for you. His name is "Lian". Show him the ropes will you?'

'Sure.'

The other men around the table watched Ludwig. He tried not to guess what they were thinking. He couldn't move.

Dr Angelus bent down and whispered in Ludwig's ear. 'Gill's a good man, *Lian*, trust him.' He then turned to Hephaestus. 'Hector, please come with me.'

The brothers glanced at each other and then Hephaestus and Dr Angelus disappeared out of the tent.

Ludwig was left alone. He turned back to the table and tried to stop himself shaking as Gill went up to him. The man clamped a hand on his shoulder before addressing his men.

'Right boys, let's be off. Lian, you're with me. We're packing up and heading off tonight. The Captain wants to be on the road before it's full dark.' He then gave Ludwig a wink and slight shove towards the kitchen. 'But you can go and grab some food first.'

Ludwig, despite his fear, didn't have to be told twice.

That evening as night fell, the Captain stood at the entrance to his tent and watched Ludwig make his way through the circus.

'They're brothers?' said Dr Angelus behind him.

'So it seems.'

'She kept that quiet.'

'Maybe, but I have a feeling even she didn't know.'

'What are we going to do with them?'

'We'll keep them here. Mandrake wants them back, or Ludwig at least, and so does her Ladyship, but it's too dangerous to go to Beacon yet so she'll just have to wait.'

'More dangerous than *here*?'

'Yeah,' said the Captain, shaking his head. 'The poor blighters.'

As the weeks passed, Ludwig got used to life in the circus. It was exhausting, but not horrible. Sometimes he talked to Hephaestus of running away, but he knew the Captain had been right. They couldn't run with Hephaestus looking the way he was. They were prisoners without a prison.

Then one evening while the circus was packing up, Ludwig looked up as he was putting away the coconut shy with Gill and saw the rest of the crew vanishing into the galley. 'What's going on?' he asked curiously.

Gill closed his crate and looked up. 'Ah,' he replied. 'You'll enjoy this. Party time.' He rubbed his hands together and smiled, 'We're goin' to have some fun owing to all the hard work we've been doing. Captain's orders.' He stood up and called out to the rest of his team. 'All right lads, get everything finished, looks like we've got the night off!'

A cheer went up and the team quickly got on with their work. But as they were packing the last of the stalls away, there was a voice nearby that made Ludwig's heart sink.

'You look like you've settled in, nice and cozy as it were.'

Ludwig and Gill turned round. Jack was there, leaning against a post and staring at them. Jack had become a plague on Ludwig's life ever since that first day he had found him in the woods. Ludwig would catch Jack staring at him, and sometimes he would walk by and whisper terrible things that kept Ludwig up at night.

'Aye Jack,' said Gill, eyeing the smaller man carefully. 'The lad's doin' well. A natural carny.'

'That's good,' Jack replied, playing with the same knife Ludwig had first seen him with. 'We don't want our new recruit not pulling his weight do we? Especially since he's been treated *so* well. Cushy job you've got here, boy. *I* never got to do the packing and the helping out when I started. I had the worst jobs I seem to recall. Seems like the Captain has taken a shine to you, as it were, and yer freak brother.'

Upon hearing the word "freak", Ludwig felt his jaw tighten, but before he could say anything, Gill took a step forward.

'He *is* young, Jack,' said Gill. 'Can't be making a young 'un do the hard stuff, he'd never cope. You were a full man when you started. And there's no need t' use language like that. If Terantless 'eard yer...'

'He and that *beast* we caught have their own quarters no less!' continued Jack, ignoring the bigger man. 'I were sleeping with the horses when I arrived.'

Gill couldn't reply to this. A few of the other crew had mentioned Ludwig and Hephaestus being given their own tent, and they weren't too happy. Ludwig had overheard them complaining when they thought he wasn't listening.

'Come on Jack,' said Gill finally. 'Let's go to the party. It'll be laugh, eh?'

'Aye Gill,' said Jack quietly. 'The party. Perhaps it *will* be fun.' He gave a short laugh and turned away.

Ludwig watched him go and Gill breathed out heavily.

'I'm sorry about Jack,' said Gill. 'He's an odd one and no mistake. You watch yourself around him, you hear? There's been incidents in the past. Nothing proved, but...'

Gill didn't need to finish his sentence, Ludwig understood.

'Why is he like that?' Ludwig asked as their team began to make their way across the circus. 'I've done nothing to him.'

'Don't matter,' replied Gill. 'A man like that don't need a reason. Poison runs through his veins. He'll go for you just for the fun of it, nothin' more.'

'Then why'd the Captain hire him?'

'Men like that can be useful I suppose. You get all sorts coming here and some can cause trouble. Having someone like Jack about evens the odds. Better the devil you know...'

'But you're hardly a coward.'

Gill smiled and patted Ludwig on the head. 'Aye, but

sometimes that ain't enough.'

Ludwig was about to ask more but he was distracted by music and singing coming out of the galley nearby. He stepped through the tent flap, and inside he was greeted by a barrage of noise. In one corner, a man was playing a fiddle and another was banging a drum in time. In the centre, men and women were dancing in a wide circle and around them people were clapping with the music. Those not dancing sat around the edges of the tent talking, drinking and laughing. It was almost deafening, and the smoke in the air made Ludwig cough.

At the far end of the tent, Ludwig saw Hephaestus sitting at one of the galley's tables talking to the other "entertainers". He waved when he caught his brother's eye.

'Ludwig!' cried Hephaestus, spotting his brother across the room. He got up and bounded across the galley. When he got to his brother, he swept him up in a mighty hug, lifting Ludwig high off the ground. After he had put Ludwig down again, the two of them, along with Gill and the rest of his team, sat down around one of the long tables.

Just then the room went quiet. Ludwig and Hephaestus looked up and saw the Captain striding across the room with Dr Angelus following behind. The Captain jumped up onto one of the tables and cupped his hands to his mouth.

'Mateys!' he cried. 'It's been a great few days. We've done well! Enjoy yourselves tonight! For tomorrow we head for new climes!'

The circus cheered as the Captain walked over to one of his men, took a flagon, and joined the dancing. Everyone clapped as they watched him swoop and swirl.

Hephaestus watched the Captain for a time, then he lent over to Gill. 'So what's the Captain's story?' he shouted over the noise.

Ludwig leaned in to listen, as did the rest of those on

the table.

'No one really knows,' shrugged Gill. 'Supposedly he used to be a, well, a "re-distributor of sea-going goods", but that was a long time ago…'

The crew looked at each other and nodded knowingly.

'A what?' said Ludwig.

' "A re-distributor. Of sea-going. Goods",' repeated Gill slowly, giving Ludwig a big wink. But seeing that Ludwig was still confused, one of the crew next to him whispered in his ear and Ludwig's eyes went wide.

'A *pirate!?*'

The table suddenly went silent. Everyone was staring. Ludwig wished he could disappear.

'Shhhh, lad!' said Gill, glancing at the Captain. 'Yeah, something like that, but he jacked it all in and started this place. Been here ever since.'

'Why?' asked Hephaestus.

'Dunno that either,' said Gill. 'Perhaps he got bored, or things got too dangerous out there. You can make a lot of enemies "*re-distributing*".'

'I heard he were made to,' said another one of Gill's team, a man called Colm who could whistle any tune you could think of. 'I 'eard he lost 'is freedom to some well-to-do woman.'

'Oh, I heard that too,' said Gill. 'But it's not likely though, is it? Nah, I think he needed to get off the oceans; too many people after him, definitely. You've seen how secretive he is? And we're *always* moving about. Can any of you remember when we were in a village more than once? He's running from something, I'm sure of it.'

Ludwig and Hephaestus exchanged glances.

'Well, we are in a circus,' said Hephaestus.

'Aye,' said Gill. 'But I've worked in a few over the years and I've never known one to travel like this one. Usually they have a few towns they'll go to over and over. But not this one. I must have seen more of Pallenway in one year with the Captain than I did in ten anywhere else.'

The other men nodded in agreement as the next round of drinks landed on the table. After that they weren't interested in talking about the Captain anymore.

A few hours later, Ludwig started to feel his eyelids grow heavy. 'I need to go to sleep,' he said, yawning.

Hephaestus nodded and the brothers got up. They said their good-nights to those on their table and left the galley and the noise behind.

'What did you think of all that?' asked Ludwig as they wandered through the circus towards their bunks. It was a moonless night and they walked slowly to avoid the tent ropes. Occasionally a snore would puncture the quiet.

'I don't know if any of it's true,' replied Hephaestus. 'But it is interesting the Captain has been moving around a lot, and before he got us too.'

'And why's he watching father? I wonder who he works for.'

Hephaestus shrugged but said nothing.

As they rounded the next tent, Hephaestus heard a cry behind him. Turning, there was Jack with his knife to Ludwig.

'Hello gents.'

'Ludwig!' cried Hephaestus, and then he realized his mistake.

'What's that, boy?' asked Jack, brushing the knife up and down Ludwig's neck. 'Your brother's got a different name has he? And here's me thinkin' it were "*Lian*".' He chuckled. 'You ain't used to this kind of place are yer? You need to be careful. *Anyone* could be listenin'.' He pressed on the knife and Ludwig yelped in pain. 'Get talkin'. What's this about the Captain and yer father? I knew something weren't right from the start, and I want to know what.'

'We were just talking, Jack, that's all,' said Ludwig as calmly as he could.

'Oh, no,' said Jack. 'I've been wonderin' about you two right from the start. And now I overhear you talking and that gets me thinkin'.'

'Let him go,' said Hephaestus, edging closer.

'In a sec, beast, in a sec. Tell me what I want to know first.'

'I–' began Hephaestus, but stopped when he looked over Jack's shoulder.

There was a click. Jack turned.

'Leave him,' said the Captain, stepping out of the darkness with a pistol raised.

'So you're even keepin' an eye on them personally now?' said Jack with a sneer. 'I *knew* it, Captain. I knew we didn't go all that way just for another work-boy and a freak. I'm not asking for much, just enough to keep my mouth shut. There's secrets here and you don't want 'em getting out, I bet.'

'Don't be daft, mate,' said the Captain. 'We were after the big one, that's all, yer know it's hard getting good entertainers. Now, put the knife down.'

'I think there's more than that. There's whisperings around the camp, as it were. Yer up to something.'

'Just put the knife *down*, mate, and we can talk.'

'Put your pistol down first.'

The Captain put the pistol on the ground. 'All right, Jack, all right, it's down.'

'Kick it over,' said Jack, and the Captain did what he was told. 'Ludwig, be a good boy and get that will you? Slowly now.' Ludwig knelt and took the gun. He could barely hold it he was shaking so hard.

'It seems like these boys know more about you than most around here, Captain. They sounded pretty definite about that—'

Ludwig was still bent down when he suddenly heard Jack cry above him. He looked up and saw his brother with his fist raised.

Jack was fast. He lashed out with his knife and Hephaestus roared in pain. But Hephaestus brought his other fist round. There was a crunch and Jack fell to the ground.

When he felt the knife leave his face, Ludwig ran. As he got to the Captain, he saw another pistol appear in the Captain's hand as if by magic.

It's okay, mate,' said the Captain, grabbing Ludwig. 'It's okay.'

'Did he hurt you?' asked Hephaestus running over to his brother. He was holding his hand to stop the blood.

Ludwig shook his head and turned to the Captain. 'I'm sorry, we—'

'It don't matter,' replied the captain, 'Keepin' yer here was always risky. Knew that from the beginning.'

'What will we do with him?' asked Hephaestus, nodding over his shoulder.

The Captain looked behind the brothers. 'With Jack? Findin' him might be a start.'

Chapter Ten:
The Greater of Two Evils

Jack seethed as he slunk out of the circus. He crept along the ditch of an unknown lane, checking behind him every few minutes to see if he was being followed. Sometimes he heard hushed voices nearby and he dropped into the mud or dived into the bushes to hide. But later, when the sun began to rise, it looked like the Captain's crew had finally given up the hunt. Jack was good at losing people if he needed to. But he also knew he wasn't safe, not yet. The Captain would come after him for what had happened; that was certain. He knew the stories about the Captain too.

However, hearing what that brat and beast were saying had been too tempting to miss. He wasn't going to hurt the boy much, just find out what he needed to know, that was all. Then the Captain appeared and ruined it, blast him! Jack spat on the ground in anger. He'd been too rash, he knew that now. If only he had taken his time. Learned more. He had been stupid and acted too soon.

As the sun started to rise overhead, Jack heard a cart rattling along the road behind him. He dived behind a hedge and peered out, but on seeing the cart wasn't from the circus, he grinned and stepped out into the lane again, waving.

'Morning squire,' he called. 'Don't suppose you would mind giving a fellow traveller a lift to the next town, as it were?'

The cart pulled up and the driver reined in his horses. The man looked at Jack carefully and then held out his hand. 'Course not. You looked like you've had a rough enough time of it already. Jump on.' The man reached out. Jack took his hand and climbed aboard. 'I'm glad of the company to be honest. It's a bit of a journey and I could do with someone to talk to.'

'Very grateful to you, squire. Very grateful,' replied Jack, still grinning his serpent grin. As the cart moved off, he felt for the knife in his pocket.

The next day, Jack cantered into the village at the end of the road. Rain beat down as he led the cart down the main street looking for the local pub. Soon enough he found it. He parked the cart and quickly made his way inside.

When he was through the pub door, he shook the water from his jacket and made his way to the bar. He dropped a coin on the counter. 'A pint,' he growled at the barkeeper.

The barkeeper nodded briefly and poured the drink without meeting Jack's eyes.

With the beer in his hand, Jack looked around for a place to sit. In one corner he spied an empty table. He made his way over to it and dropped himself down in a chair, making those near him look at him suspiciously before they carried on with what they were doing.

As he drank, Jack listened to the conversations. Most were dull, about local things he couldn't care less about. Then one caught his attention.

'I heard it were a monster.' said one man. He sipped on the drink in his hand and wiped his mouth with this cuff. 'They say it took a boy and ran off into the local woods. Never seen again. The boy neither.'

'A terrible thing,' said the other. 'Imagine that, a monster loose in Pallenway.'

'His father's frantic so I heard... and rich too. Some sir or other.'

'Oh yeah?' said the other.

'Yeah, he lives in a village called Little Wandswell or something.'

'Ah,' the second man sighed. 'That must be miles away.'

Jack couldn't believe his luck! Too many bells were ringing for him to ignore. 'Excuse me gents,' he began. 'I couldn't help but overhear your conversation, as it were.'

The two men looked up at the stranger nervously. 'Not polite to listen to others talk, you know,' said the first.

'Apologies gents, apologies, but hearing about monsters can attract the ear. How about I buy you two a drink and you can tell me all about it?'

The two men looked at each other and shrugged. 'Fair enough,' said the first. 'Can't refuse a drink can we, Harold?' The other man shook his head.

Jack ran to the bar and came back with three more mugs of thick beer. 'Now, I don't suppose you know when this terrible crime took place?' he asked once he was sitting down again.

'Couple of months back, so I heard,' said the first man.

'Really, that *is* interesting, that is. And this town you mentioned. It wasn't called something like Little Wainesford now, was it?'

'Aye, that's the place! Little Wainesford! I remember clear as day now. Some bloke called von Guggenstein. He's the father. Ha! Where have you been? I'm surprised you don't know about it already. It's been the talk of the town for about a week or so. Most of Pallenway must have heard about it by now–'

Jack stared at the man, then got up and ran out of the pub.

'He's left his drink,' said the first man.

The circus packed up and left the morning after Jack's attack. No one knew what happened, but on seeing Jack had disappeared, there was now a good feeling in the air, like a cloud has blown away and it was light again.

Ludwig and Hephaestus soon got back to work. However, Hephaestus was taken out of the entertainers' tent and told to help look after the animals instead; away from the eyes of any visiting villagers and townsfolk that might be wandering around.

The Captain also started spending much more time with the brothers. Occasionally, when they had finished their work early and it was not yet time to open, he would take them out fishing or for a walk nearby. He rarely let them out his sight.

'The Captain's worried,' said Hephaestus one day as the brothers sat with fishing poles in their hands, watching water-boatmen flit across an unnamed river.

'I know,' replied Ludwig. 'I think Jack really scared him.'

The brothers turned to look at the Captain. He was looking out onto the river most of the time, but the brothers could see his eyes dart to the riverbank every once in a while, searching the bushes and trees. His pistols were always in his belt these days.

'Any luck, mates?' The Captain called out when he caught the brothers looking at him.

'Not yet,' Hephaestus called back trying to sound relaxed. Ludwig just shook his head.

'No matter. Pack up yer things. The sun's goin' down. Time to get to work.'

Jack got to Little Wainesford in a few days. He rode his horse to death and slept only when he had to, so desperate was he to get to the village. But as he passed the first houses on the outskirts, he noticed something was wrong. Little Wainesford was deathly quiet. Doors creaked in the breeze and sometimes Jack thought he caught the sound of a lonely dog barking. There were none of the normal village sounds. No voices chatting away. No banging and clanking from the blacksmith's. No women gossiping over fences. Little Wainesford was empty.

Strange.

At the church, he stopped and rested against the graveyard wall. He picked one of the blue flowers that were growing there and crushed it between his fingers, throwing it to the ground in frustration. He was about to set off again and search through the houses to see if there was anything to steal (to make the trip at least somewhat worthwhile), but something caught his eye.

On a path going out of the village, something moved. Jack looked hard. Someone was coming towards him. It was difficult to be sure, but it looked like a small, hunched old woman.

Jack brushed himself down and began walking towards the woman with a smile on his face, waving to get her attention. As he got closer, he saw the old woman was wearing a dirty cloak that covered her entire body. It looked like it could have even been just a cut sack. He noticed she moved in strange, jerking steps, and a high-pitched whine came from under her clothes. Jack was not normally afraid (it was he who usually made others afraid after all), but something about this creature sent a shiver down his spine. *It's just an old woman,* he thought, but he put his hand in his pocket to feel the reassuring handle of his knife just in case.

'Greetin's,' Jack called out when the woman was closer.

'I need to speak with someone called Guggenstein. I'm 'ere about the kidnappin'. I might be able to help the gentleman find his son, as it were.'

The woman didn't reply. She just kept walking towards him and the whining got louder.

'Did yer hear me?' asked Jack, trying to sound as friendly as he could.

When she got closer, he noticed he couldn't see her face under the cloak; the folds covered it completely. He wondered how she knew where she was going.

'I'm just trying to help.' He said reassuringly. He tried to give her a winning smile but she ignored him. There was a faint scratching sound and she raised her arm. Poking out of the cloak was a piece of slate with writing on it. Jack took it and read:

FOLLOW.

'Er… as yer wish,' he replied, handing the slate back.

The woman turned and walked away without saying a word. Jack followed behind.

They made their way up the path, away from the village. Ahead, Jack saw a small castle appearing through the trees.

The father's rich…

When they arrived, the gates swung open and they walked on through into a courtyard. At the entrance, the old woman stopped and opened the new-looking front door. Finally, she stepped to one side and handed Jack the slate again.

ENTER.

Jack did as he was told. When he was on the other side of the door, he gazed up and whistled loudly. He found himself in a grand hall; full of things that shined and looked *very* expensive.

He followed the woman up the main staircase and they came to a set of doors. Behind them he heard music playing. The old woman pushed one of the doors open and let Jack through.

Inside, Jack found what appeared to be a library. As he passed the shelves full of books, he looked around.

The clever sort, he thought to himself. *This'll be easy.*

Soon enough, Jack found his host. Mandrake sat at his piano and ignored Jack completely. Jack, who cared little for music, gave a loud cough.

'Excuse me sir,' he called out. 'I was shown here by your good woman. Would you be... er... von Guggenstein?'

Mandrake stopped and looked puzzled. 'My good woman? Ah, you mean...' He closed the piano lid. 'I am he. However I would prefer you addressed me as "Professor von Guggenstein", or "sir".'

'Ah, right, right you are, "*sir*".'

'And you wish to speak to me about...?'

'Well, I hear yer son's gone missin' and I think I might be able to help yer out, as it were.'

Mandrake turned to face Jack. 'You have found Ludwig,' he asked without emotion.

'Ludwig, aye, that's him. He's been calling himself something different though.'

'Are you sure you have the right boy? Tell me what you know or leave. I've had too many time-wasters already.'

Jack heard the door crack open behind him. 'Hold on there, sir, I *do* know him, I'm sure of it. Took by a monster right? I know where *he* is too.'

'Go on.'

'We– I mean *I,* I came across 'em a while back. Miles from here. I remember thinkin', "they're a strange pair and no mistake." Then I heard about the kidnapping and put two and two together. I thought it must be them! Don't think young lads and monsters walkin' around together is a common occurrence in Pallenway.' Jack smiled to himself. He had got this Guggenstein's attention now.

'Where are they?'

'Well, I want to tell you, I really do. Nothing would make me happier than bringin' a father back together with his long lost son, but, well, I have kids to feed...'

'Of course. You want a reward.'

Jack laughed to himself. That's the rich for you, all caring and desperate when they need to be, but mention money and they're hard as stone.

Mandrake went over to his desk and opened a drawer. 'Allow me to offer you something for your troubles. Ten Scetans should be sufficient.'

Ten Scetans! thought Jack. *That's nothing these days. However...*

'You know, sir. It's not my business to pry, but when I heard about the kidnapping, I thought to myself, Jack, something doesn't make sense here. You know what I mean?'

Mandrake paused. 'No.'

'Really? Well, sir if I may, that *is* a surprise. You see, when I found... Ludwig? Is that right? He didn't seem kidnapped to me. He and that...freak seemed quite friendly with each other, as it were. Called themselves brothers. Did you know that?'

'Indeed? Brothers you say?'

'Indeed, sir, indeed. Quite friendly. And they had made up these fake names to boot. So I start to think, Jack, perhaps this son of the fine gentleman isn't so much kidnapped, as it were. Perhaps he's *running* from something, and perhaps the freak isn't so much a kidnapper, but a fellow escapee.'

'Oh,' said Mandrake, raising an eyebrow.

'Well sir, it's not my place to poke my nose into someone

else's business...'

'But?'

'"But!" Ha! Yes, you're sharp there, sir. *But,* as I said, I've a wife and kids to feed...'

Mandrake closed the drawer, sat down in his chair and looked at Jack. 'No, I don't think so.'

'I *am* surprised you'd say that, sir.' Jack took his knife out of his pocket and started toying with it. 'I don't suppose I could ask you to reconsider? I doubt you'd want people knowing what I know now, do you?'

Mandrake sighed. 'You're trying to blackmail me.' It wasn't a question.

'Blackmail? Well, now you mention it...' Jack leered. He was good at leering.

'Do you want to know something?'

Jack paused. This wasn't how it usually went. The man should be scared by now. They were *always* scared by now. Jack was much bigger than this von Guggenstein, and could break him without much effort. But he just sat there, calm as anything.

'I'll tell you anyway,' Mandrake continued. 'It's people like you that have rotted this country, have made it weak. Everywhere I look, there are cowards and the corrupt. I despair, I really do.' Mandrake lent back in his chair, making it creak. 'However, thankfully, you can be redeemed.'

Jack suddenly realised he had never heard the door to the library close again. But before he could turn, something had hit him hard and he crashed down on the floor. Moments later, a weight pressed down on his back, almost crushing him, and he could hear that horrible whining sound again. That blasted old woman was on him and she was a lot heavier than he thought! He managed to turn his head and he saw Mandrake rise from his chair out of the corner of his eye.

'Do you know how many people have come here looking

for money?' said Mandrake, bending down so Jack could see him clearly. 'They are usually just drifters, or people trying to take advantage of a desperate situation, but knowing nothing. *You* are different, I can tell. You *do* know my boy, I'm sure. However, you are also greedy, and dared to threaten me with violence in my own house. I think you would have actually carried out your threat too had it not been for...what was it now? "My good woman?" Mandrake studied Jack. 'There is poison in your veins,' he muttered, 'but perhaps even poison can be used for good.'

'Get 'er off me!' Jack cried out.

'I don't think so,' replied Mandrake.

A few days later...

'Run over and find Hettie for me, would you love? She's got my tarot cards. I need 'em for the punters.'

Ludwig nodded to Madame Esbella and ran out of her trailer. It was getting dark when he stepped outside, and those who would be visiting the circus would be here soon. Madame Esbella was the last person he had to see before the circus opened and, apart from her missing cards, it looked like everything was ready for a good show.

He jumped down the steps and ran off towards the galley, fairly sure Hettie, Madame Esbella's assistant, would be there grabbing a last bite to eat. But as he ran round a cart, he crashed straight into someone. He fell to the floor, dazed. 'I'm sorry,' Ludwig managed, 'I wasn't looking where I was going–'

'You always were a clumsy boy.'

Ludwig looked up. His father stood there, towering over him.

'Hello boy. I see you are keeping well.'

Before his father could say anything more, Ludwig scrabbled to his feet and ran. He shot through the circus, blindly bumping into customers and crew alike. He didn't dare turn back. He rounded the main tent, jumping over the guide ropes that blocked his path, and saw Hephaestus helping take the elephants back to their cages. 'Hephaestus!' he cried. 'He's here!'

Hephaestus stopped what he was doing and looked up. 'Who? Jack?!'

'No!' said Ludwig, white as a sheet. 'Father!'

Hephaestus looked past Ludwig and saw his father striding through the crowd. When Ludwig got to him, he grabbed his brother and pulled him out of the way.

'Don't come any closer!' Hephaestus cried out.

'Hephaestus, my boy,' said Mandrake softly. 'I am so glad I have found you.'

'Captain!' Hephaestus bellowed, ignoring his father. 'Captain!'

'Please, listen to me, my boy. Stop shouting like that. Let us talk. What happened before was a… misunderstanding, that's all. I was angry and acted rashly.'

'I don't believe you,' said Hephaestus, quickly looking around. 'Captain!' he cried out again. 'Where are you!'

Around them, a crowd started to gather.

'Hephaestus, you must listen. I didn't mean for what happened to happen. I was under a lot of pressure…it was silly. Let us forget about it. Please, come home.'

Ludwig peered around his brother and he caught his father's eye. His father bent down and leaned towards him with his arms outstretched.

'Please, Ludwig I want you, *both* of you, to return to the castle. Live proper lives again.'

'Maybe–' began Ludwig, looking up at his brother.

'He's lying,' said Hephaestus, pushing Ludwig back

behind him. 'Remember what happened.'

'I'm not, I swear,' replied Mandrake. 'Come back and you'll see. I've had to do some things that you may not like but...they were necessary.' He looked desperately at his sons. 'I'm changing the world for the better my boys, I've found my calling, and I want you two to be part of that.'

'You were going to shoot me,' said Hephaestus.

'I wasn't thinking properly, child. I understand I was wrong and I'm sorry, but we need to put it in the past and move on.'

'How did you find us?' asked Ludwig.

'A man came to visit me one day. He was very helpful.'

'Jack...' said Ludwig.

'Jack? Was that his name? A rough type. He would look at home in this place.' Mandrake waved his hand around with a look of disgust on his face. 'I put out a reward for you and he came out of the woodwork. Quite a horrendous person truth be told.'

'Is... is he here?' Ludwig's eyes darted around, peering into the crowd.

'No. I would *never* let someone like that near you.'

Ludwig was about to take a step forward when he heard someone come up behind him. He felt a hand on his shoulder.

'Don't, mate.'

Ludwig looked up and saw the Captain with his pistol drawn.

'How dare you!' snarled Mandrake. 'Take your hands off him this instant!'

'I'm not giving him to yer, Mandrake. I'll kill yer right in front of him rather than the lad fall into your hands again.'

'What? Do I *know* you?' seethed Mandrake. Frustration rang through his voice.

'No, but it don't matter.' The Captain turned to

Hephaestus. 'Go to the back of my tent, you'll find a carriage and a couple of horses. Get them ready. Quickly now!'

'This is ridiculous,' said Mandrake. 'Hephaestus, ignore him. Let's get this all sorted out, away from people like this. How you've ended up here I don't know, but you can tell me all about it on the ride home–'

'Don't listen to him,' said the Captain. 'Run.'

'But–'

'Go!'

Hephaestus looked at his father, then backed away and started running towards the Captain's tent.

Mandrake watched him go and sighed. 'So much promise...,' he muttered to himself. Then he turned to the Captain and Ludwig. 'I don't have the patience for this. Too many fools, just too many fools.' He reached into his pocket, took out something small and lifted it to his mouth.

Moments later screams could be heard from the other side of the circus. Only a few at first, but they grew in number, louder and louder. Then there was a terrible, familar sound.

Eeeeeeeeeeeeeeeeeeeeeeeee!

Ludwig stared wide-eyed as the whining got closer. 'You didn't destroy it.'

'Of course not,' said Mandrake dismissively. 'If you're not coming, then I have no choice but to do this. You never make it easy do you, boy? In future I expect you to be more obedient.'

Ludwig turned away and saw a flash of metal in the crowd. 'Captain?' he said, tugging on his jacket.

'What's going on, mate?'

'We need to run,' pleaded Ludwig quietly, terrified.

'Why?'

'He has a machine. It can do things.'

'Don't worry, lad. I know how tricky yer father can be.

I've got a fair few men here. I think we can handle whatever he's got.'

Ludwig heard clicking behind him.

'Aye boy,' came the voice of Gill. He and his team had appeared. 'You're not going any place you don't want to.'

'No Captain, Gill, please listen. You'll die,' replied Ludwig, hearing the screaming getting closer and closer. 'It's not just... we need to run.' Ludwig tried to pull away but the Captain held him tight. He turned and saw people fleeing in every direction. The crowd parted and standing there was the HELOT. It stopped when it caught sight of his father.

'Take the boy. Kill the rest,' said Mandrake.

The HELOT turned and launched itself at Gill. Gill lifted his gun and tried to fire, but the machine was too fast. Its claws tore into him and he cried out, trying to push the HELOT back with his hands alone. But it was no use. The machine was too strong and it was over quickly. When it was done with Gill, the HELOT stepped over his body and looked at the Captain.

'My god...' The Captain raised his pistol and fired off a shot. The bullet hit the HELOT and it flew back, leaving a gaping hole where one of its eyes used to be. It lay on the ground, not moving. The Captain then lowered his gun and looked at Gill's body.

'He were a good man, Mandrake. You'll suffer for this.' He pulled the second pistol out of his belt and pulled its hammer back. 'I were told to not hurt yer, but now...'

Mandrake didn't reply. Instead, he pointed into the crowd.

'Oh, no,' whispered Ludwig. Beyond, another HELOT was pushing its way through the circus-goers. It moved quickly, knocking down anyone in its way. Then another appeared, then another, and another, and another.

'Go lad!' cried the Captain. He pushing Ludwig away and

they both started running. Behind them, they could hear the HELOTs coming after them.

Ludwig heard another shot echo into the night. More people screamed.

'It looks like your father's been busy!' said the Captain as they got to his tent. Ludwig just nodded. He couldn't speak.

Behind the tent, they found Hephaestus stepping into a carriage, the horses ready to go. The Captain jumped onto the box, grabbed the reins, and snapped them to get the horses moving as Ludwig dived into the cabin after his brother.

In the carriage, Ludwig and Hephaestus looked up as part of the roof slid open and the Captain's head appeared.

'Ludwig,' he called out. 'I need yer up here!'

Ludwig stepped underneath the hatch and Hephaestus took him by the waist and lifted him up. When he got outside, he scrambled onto the carriage's box while the Captain reached under the seat and took out a shoebox. He passed it to Ludwig.

'Open it,' said the Captain.

Inside, Ludwig found a pile of pistols. He took one out gingerly, as if it were about to bite him.

'Don't be nervous. Just point it and shoot, then throw it down the hatch.' The Captain took another smaller box and threw it down to Hephaestus. '*You* need to reload 'em. Can yer do that?'

'I think so,' replied Hephaestus over the noise of the carriage.

'Ludwig, shoot those things now!' cried the Captain.

Ludwig looked up and saw the HELOTs coming at them. Their legs pumped up and down and clumps of grass were thrown up with each step. Their speed was incredible.

He pointed the pistol and pulled the trigger. It fired with

a bang and his arms flew upwards. Pain shot through his shoulders and hands, but when he opened his eyes again, he saw one of the HELOTs lying on the ground.

'Good lad!' said the Captain, slapping Ludwig hard on the back. 'Now get another!'

Ludwig threw the pistol to his brother and picked up a second. He aimed and fired again. Another HELOT went down. He and the Captain cheered. He had managed to keep his eyes open this time. As the carriage sped up, Ludwig managed to hit five more. Soon they were slowly dropping away.

'We made it–' said Ludwig, but before he could finish, another HELOT burst out of the bushes and smashed into the side of the carriage. The carriage tipped it on to two wheels before it came crashing back down onto four.

When Ludwig had regained his footing, he peered over the side. The machine was holding on, clawing its way up towards him; wood splintering under its grip. He reached down to take another pistol, but they were gone.

No ...

He glanced over the other side of the carriage and saw the box on the ground, disappearing as they rolled on. 'No,' he moaned. 'Captain-' But as he felt his heart sink, the door to the carriage swung open and Hephaestus appeared.

Hephaestus reached out, grabbed one of the machine's legs and pulled just as its claws bit into the edge of the carriage right next to his brother's feet.

The HELOT made a screeching sound as its mechanisms resisted, but Hephaestus had the advantage. He pulled again and the machine fell away. It soared through the air, smashing hard into a passing tree, and there was an almighty crash as it crumpled up against the trunk.

The Captain whipped the horses and they fled.

Chapter Eleven:
Beacon

Later, the Captain slowed the horses and let them rest after their run. They were far away from the terror of the circus now, but Ludwig watched as the Captain's eyes darted this way and that, still on guard. Occasionally there would be a noise and the Captain's hands would go to his pistols, but nothing jumped out at them. It seemed safe for the time being.

'That was close,' said Ludwig as an owl hooted in a nearby tree.

'Aye mate.' said the Captain. He shook his head. 'I didn't think Mandrake would find you at the circus. I never expected that.'

'What will we do now?'

The Captain lent back. 'We can't go back, that's for certain. But Beacon's close enough. We can get there in a day or so if we hurry. That'll be best.'

Ludwig was surprised. While in the circus, they had stayed away from anything bigger than a village. Beacon was huge and full of people.

'Why there?'

'It's where my employer lives.'

'And who would that be?' Hephaestus called out from inside the carriage.

'You'll find out soon enough,' replied the Captain.

Ludwig was too tired to argue. He crawled into the carriage to try to get some sleep.

After hours had passed, Ludwig woke to a knocking on the roof.

'I'm awake,' he called out. The hatch above him opened and the Captain's face appeared.

'We're here boys.'

Ludwig yawned and then sniffed the air. He grimaced, wrinkling his nose in disgust. It smelt awful. 'Urgh! What's *that?*'

'Beacon,' said the Captain cheerfully. 'Put enough people in one place and it's going to smell pretty fragrant. Come and have a look.'

Ludwig lifted his head off Hephaestus' lap and climbed up out through the hatch. Outside, he sat down in wonder. All around them, he saw carts and people on foot wandering in both directions. His eyes followed the road. On the horizon, he spotted what must be Beacon.

'There', said the Captain, pointing. 'Impressive, ain't it?'

Beacon sprawled over the landscape like a great dark wave. On one side of the city, chimneys shot up into the clouds, belching black smoke that stained the sky. The rest of the city was a jumble of dirty, whitewashed, wooden, and stone buildings thrown together and built on top of one another in all shapes and sizes. They were packed in so closely Ludwig couldn't help but wonder how people got from one place to another without walking through someone else's home.

'It's huge,' he said, impressed.

'Aye, it's one of the bigger cities,' agreed the Captain. 'There are a few larger, but not many.'

Behind them, Hephaestus poked his head through the hatch. 'I think I should stay out of sight.'

'Good idea mate. With Mandrake looking for both of you, you'd best to keep yer head down.'

As the carriage got to Beacon's outskirts, Ludwig stared fascinated at the people walking and riding by.

Some nodded as they passed while others made every effort not to pay them any attention, but almost all of them looked so different from anyone Ludwig had met before in his short life. Women in great, blooming dresses were carefully perched on top of proud horses; their husbands and servants were beside them, all looking very smart. Around their feet, small children of no more than five or six ran around kicking a ball between them, dressed in nothing but torn and dirty rags. Ludwig watched them all as he entered into the city.

'This is Thelick Street,' said the Captain pointing down the huge through-way that seemed to cut the city in half. 'Yer can get all the way to the docks followin' it. Over there,' he pointed his finger to a larger building poking up over the roofs, 'is the old Superbus' palace, but it's more of a museum than anything else nowadays. And over there is the council house, and opposite, Beacon Cathedral.' They carried on for almost an hour with the Captain pointing out the sights. 'Ah, and this is where we need to be,' he said finally.

The carriage turned off the main street and into what looked like a wealthy part of town.

Minutes later, they pulled up outside one of the sets of gates built into the high walls surrounding one of the houses. The Captain jumped off the carriage, rang a bell, and a small slit in the gate opened up.

'It's me. Let us in.'

The slit closed again and the gate creaked open. The Captain jumped back on the carriage and they drove through.

Behind the gates was a huge, white mansion. On top of the mansion steps stood a tall old man dressed in black. He watched stony-faced as the carriage pulled up in front of him.

'And where is the third, sir?' asked the man after his eyes had flicked over Ludwig and the Captain.

'Inside mate,' replied the Captain. 'Hephaestus!'

The door to the carriage opened and Hephaestus climbed out. Ludwig noticed the man's eyes widen slightly, but otherwise he didn't show any sign of surprise.

'Come this way, please.' The man turned and walked inside.

The Captain looked at the brothers and winked. 'Best behaviour now gents. You ain't among rogues any more.'

The man in black took the three travelers through the main entrance of the house and into a waiting room. Inside were wide, cushioned chairs where the man told the Captain, Ludwig and Hephaestus to sit.

'Wait here please. I will—'

'Don't worry Gransfarn,' came a woman's voice. 'I'm here.'

The man in black turned and bowed. 'Of course, madam.'

Ludwig looked past the man and saw the woman who spoke. She was very tall and very old, with grey hair tightly pulled back to a bun at the back of her head. She was dressed in clothes that he guessed were very expensive. Her eyes flashed to him and she gasped. 'Oh my!' she cried out and dropped into a chair.

The man in black quickly rushed over to her. 'Madame? Are you well? May I get you anything?'

'No no, Gransfarn. I'm fine. Thank you.' She looked up and caught Ludwig's eye again. 'I was surprised, that's all.'

'Perhaps I should wait in the carriage,' Hephaestus mumbled uncomfortably. He stood up and was about to walk out when the old woman stopped him.

'No. It's not you my dear. Please stay.' She stood up and

walked over to Ludwig, studying his face closely by taking hold of his chin with her fingers. She turned his head to one side then the other.

'I'm sorry. You remind me a great deal of someone I used to know.'

Ludwig fidgeted uncomfortably in his chair, not knowing what to say.

'Are you the person who employs the Captain?' asked Hephaestus.

The woman turned to him and gave out a small laugh. 'Yes, I suppose I am.' She then looked at the Captain. 'Thank you for bringing them to me.'

'M'lady,' he replied, nodding his head.

'Who *are* you?' asked Hephaestus.

'I—' She paused. 'My name is Matilda von Guggenstein. I'm your grandmother.' Ludwig and Hephaestus stared at her in disbelief.

'What?' the brothers said together.

'I'm sorry,' she smiled. 'It seems to be one shock after another this morning.'

'*You've* been the one watching father?' asked Ludwig.

'Yes.'

'He never said anything about you,' said Ludwig, suspiciously.

'I don't suppose he would. We haven't seen each other for years.' She reached around her neck and took the locket hanging there. She clicked it open and passed it to Hephaestus, dropping it into his massive palm.

Hephaestus looked surprised. 'You'd better see this,' he said to his brother.

Ludwig took the locket. On one of the panels was a picture of a younger version of their father. He must have been only sixteen years old or so. It was strange to see him so young. On the other was a picture of another familiar-looking man. Ludwig peered closer and gasped. 'It's me!' he said. 'But how–'

'No,' said Matilda softly. 'That's Louis, my late husband. That's why I was so shocked when I first saw you. That photograph was taken around the time I met him for the very first time. He would have been only a year or two older than you are now. You could be twins.'

Ludwig stood up and walked over to the woman. She looked at him with concern, but then Ludwig lent forward and wrapped his arms around her. 'Thank you for rescuing us.'

'My pleasure!' she replied, laughing in surprise. 'You have no idea how much I have been looking forward to today.'

As the evening drew in, Ludwig and Hephaestus told Matilda about their lives until Ludwig could no longer keep his eyes open. When he started slumping on his chair, Hephaestus lifted him up in his arms and said good night to the Captain and his grandmother.

The Captain watched Hephaestus and Ludwig follow the butler to bed. After he heard the last creak of the stairs, he put down his drink and turned to Matilda. 'So they definitely are yours?' he asked.

'I can't be certain. Even with Ludwig looking so much like Louis…' The happiness of the evening started to fade from her face.

'But Mandrake having kids? From what yer've told me, he doesn't seem the type to have started a family, especially after that business in Juleto. I know he disappeared for a while, but still…'

'We must face facts,' Matilda replied. 'I've no reason to doubt them. We have found each other and that's all that matters, and I will care for them as long as I am able. I don't know what Mandrake is doing but I don't want them involved.' She yawned. 'It's late Captain, and I need to sleep. Tomorrow we are leaving. Mandrake won't know I've got the boys, but it may not take him long to work it out.'

The Captain nodded and said nothing more.

'Gransfarn has prepared your usual room and a crew has been assembled for tomorrow. A few of your old crew are even still around. Good night.'

The Captain stood up and watched her leave. 'Thank you. 'Night, M'lady.' Then he took his chair and pulled it round so it faced the fire. He stared into the flames, lost in thought.

Chapter Twelve:
Voyage

Ludwig was already up and dressed when he heard the knock on the door from Gransfarn the next morning.

'Young master?' the old butler called from the outside.

'Come in Gransfarn. I'm awake.'

'No need young sir. Come down as soon as possible. We will be departing soon and you must eat.'

'I'll be there in a bit.'

'Very well,' the old butler replied, and Ludwig heard him walk away.

Ludwig walked over to the window and looked over the path that led away from the house. Below him were two carriages, much grander than the one they had arrived in, being loaded with suitcases by people he didn't recognise.

There was another knock on his door. This one was much heavier than the butler's.

'Come in, Hephaestus.'

Hephaestus opened the door and stepped inside. He was dressed in new clothes and looked clean and fresh.

'Did you sleep well?' he asked.

'The best I've done for a while.'

Hephaestus walked over to the bed and sat down. 'It looks like we're moving again.'

Ludwig nodded. 'I saw. Do you know where we're going?'

Hephaestus shook his head. 'No, but by the look of it we're not coming back, at least not for a while. Servants are putting covers on the furniture.'

Ludwig looked out of the window while his brother spoke and saw the gate at the far end of the garden open. Through it came another carriage followed by a man on horseback. He watched the carriage and rider come up the drive, and soon the rider's face came into view.

'Hephaestus!' shouted Ludwig, excitedly. 'It's Dr Angelus!'

Ludwig ran out of the room with Hephaestus lumbering behind. When they got to the front door, they found the Captain grasping his first mate warmly by the hand. Beside them was Matilda looking happy.

'Viktor,' she said warmly. 'The Captain told me what happened. We had feared the worst.'

'Aye mate,' said the Captain. 'You've no idea how relieved I am to see yer.'

Dr Angelus shook the Captain's hand. 'Sir, Madam. I was lucky that's all.'

'You don't have to call us that here,' said the Captain. Then he paused. 'What about the others? Did they get away?'

'As far as I know, I was the only one. I'm sorry, Captain.'

The Captain forced a smile. 'It's terrible, just terrible, but you're alive and that's some consolation. Come on inside and get some breakfast inside yer.'

'Certainly, but I have something to show you first.' Dr Angelus walked back to the carriage and opened the door.

Inside, there was a creaking as something moved in the darkness. Ludwig walked passed the Captain and his grandmother to get a better view.

'Hello lad,' came a voice from within.

Ludwig gasped. 'Mr Shawlworth?'

The gardener stepped out of the carriage with a broad grin on his face. Ludwig ran over to him and hugged the old gardener tightly. 'I thought I'd never see you again! Or anyone from back home! What are you doing here? How is everyone? How's Mrs Pewsnitt? And-' Ludwig poured out his questions without breath, but he stopped when he saw the look on his friend's face.

'Let's go inside,' said the gardener, quietly. 'Everyone needs to hear this.'

They went to the dining room and sat down. Moments later, servants came in, placed the breakfast on the table, and left as quickly as they entered. Finally, Mr Shawlworth spoke.

'Terrible things happened after you left lad,' he began after he had a sip of his coffee. 'When you and… Hephaestus? Is that right? Yes? When you two were seen that night, the villagers were furious. They marched to the castle and demanded to see your father. After what happened with Mr Pewsnitt… well, they wanted blood.'

'I imagine they got it,' said Ludwig's grandmother, quietly.

Mr Shawlworth hung his head. Ludwig could see he was very upset.

'Go on,' said Ludwig quietly. 'What happened?'

'They got to the castle and found the gates broken down. They went inside and searched everywhere, desperate to find your father, but he'd vanished.'

'He's good at that,' muttered the Captain.

'Thinking he'd run off out of shame, they left the castle and went back to the village. There wasn't much else they could do other than hope your father wouldn't come back and his monster would leave them alone.' Mr Shawlworth then rubbed his brow. 'And… that's when the disappearances started. One night, a few days later, a couple of people went missing: Mr Jameson and Mr Huddlekin.'

Ludwig recognised both their names.

'No one thought about it at first,' said the gardener. 'Everyone guessed they were ill, but the next day…' he looked at Ludwig. 'Do you remember Bernard, lad?'

'Yes…' replied Ludwig, remembering the boy who had come to the castle when Mr Pewsnitt died.

'He was one of the next to go, amongst others. We went round to their homes, but they had disappeared.'

'Oh, no,' whispered Ludwig.

'We were terrified. We thought it was the Professor's monster coming for us. We had a meeting that day, trying to decide what to do next and…' The old man was holding back tears. 'And that's when they attacked.'

Those around the table looked at Mr Shawlworth sadly.

'We couldn't do anything,' said the gardener. 'Those…'

'HELOTs,' said Ludwig.

'Is that what they're called? HELOTS? They ran at us while we were talking, grabbing people and pulling them off towards the castle. Those who weren't caught fled but… I don't think anyone else made it. I hid in the woods and kept myself out of sight. The others weren't so lucky.' Ludwig's grandmother walked over to Mr Shawlworth and wrapped her arms around him. 'Oh, Matilda,' the gardener whispered. 'It were awful.'

Matilda turned to Ludwig and his brother. 'Do you have *any* idea what he's doing?' she asked sternly.

Ludwig shook his head.

'I do,' Hephaestus rumbled.

Ludwig turned and stared at his brother.

'Tell us child,' said Matilda softly.

Hephaestus took a deep breath. 'Father needs people for the machines,' he explained. 'He takes a piece of their minds and puts it inside them. It means they can work on their own.'

'That's not how they work,' said Ludwig, surprised. 'They

use a box–'

'About this big?' replied Hephaestus. 'Has lights shining inside?' He moved his hands into a shape that would have fitting the cube Ludwig had been shown.

'But–'

There was a cough from the other end of the table. Dr Angelus put down his glass. 'If this is true, he's getting people outside your village too. I stayed at the circus for a while after the attack. I saw the HELOTs carrying people away.'

'That's awful!' gasped Matilda, putting her hand over her mouth. 'Those poor people.'

'By Azmon!' cried the Captain. 'I'll string him up!'

'I'm sorry,' said Hephaestus, lowering his eyes. 'He told me once. He said he would never actually do it. He promised…'

'That's why,' muttered Ludwig. 'In the library…' He quickly got up and ran out of the room as fast as he could.

'I'll talk to him,' said Hephaestus.

Hephaestus found Ludwig lying on his bed, his face pushed into his pillow. Hephaestus walked over to the bed, sat down, and placed a heavy hand on his brother's back.

'Ludwig, I…' he began, searching for the right words. 'I didn't mean to lie to you.'

'So that's why you were angry with father, and *that's* why he tried to… do what he was going to do,' Ludwig's voice was muffled by the pillow.

'Yes, I didn't know what to say to you afterwards. It never seemed the right time, and the more I waited the harder it got. I thought…I thought you'd hate me.'

Ludwig rolled over. 'Why?' he said quietly,

'Because you already felt guilty enough for Mr Pewsnitt.'

'What's that got to do—' Then it dawned on him. 'Oh no. Please...'

'I think he was the first.'

Ludwig didn't say anything more. He curled up against his brother and cried. They sat, not speaking for a while, until there was a gentle knock at the door.

'Young masters,' came the voice of Gransfarn quietly. 'Please come down. We are leaving.'

Ludwig and Hephaestus looked at each other. Then Ludwig quickly wiped his eyes with the cuff of his shirt and they left the room. Nothing more needed to be said.

'Captain,' said Matilda when Ludwig and Hephaestus appeared outside. 'You and Hephaestus come with me. Everyone else, take the second carriage. Our ship is at the docks ready to set sail.'

They piled into the waiting carriages and minutes later they were on Beacon's streets. As they trundled on, Ludwig lent out of the carriage to get a better view and to clear his head after all he had learned.

At first they passed wealthy-looking houses, but as they got further away from his grandmother's home, the buildings got smaller and less well-kept. Soon they were in an area very different from before. The houses nearby looked broken-down; and in between were dark alleys where shrouded people glanced at them suspiciously before disappearing into darkness, despite the light of morning.

'We're in Tasek town now,' said Mr Shawlworth. 'It's pretty dangerous around here. Don't lean too far out, lad. You might not come back.'

Ludwig sat back into his seat and Mr Shawlworth smiled at him. 'Her ladyship won't be too happy if she loses you again after all this time.'

'Why didn't you tell me about grandmother when I was back home?' asked Ludwig.

'She didn't want me to tell you about her, and I had to respect her wishes.'

'How do you know her?'

'I've been in Little Wainesford a long time and I knew Matilda when she lived there in her younger days. We were friends and sent each other letters occasionally after she had left. Once, she sent me a letter asking me to meet her after Mandrake returned to the castle. You were just a baby then. I came to Beacon and she said she wanted me to keep an eye on you and him, that's all. When she asked me, I thought she was worrying over her son like all mothers do. I didn't think there was anything sinister about it. Although I did think it was strange she never came to visit. As time went on she told me more about the fears she had over Mandrake. Soon enough, I was introduced to Viktor here, who would take my letters and deliver hers.'

Ludwig huffed and crossed his arms.

'Sorry lad, I didn't want to keep secrets from you, but I promised.'

The carriage was silent as the decrepit houses disappeared and warehouses took their place. When the warehouses stopped, Ludwig suddenly saw the sea.

Not wanting to talk any more, he jumped out of the carriage as it came to a stop and ran to the edge of the docks, to a spot where there wasn't a ship or people blocking his view. He stared out, watching the water ripple and glisten as the sun shone down. Below, he saw small fish darting around underwater, and nearby, ships bobbed and banged against the piers. He had never seen the ocean before.

'You'll be on it soon enough mate,' said the Captain coming up behind him. 'Come and have a look at this.'

Ludwig turned and the Captain pointed at a huge ship gently rising up and down on the waves. 'That's mine,' said Tom.

'It's got sails!' said Ludwig in surprise. 'I didn't think their *were* ships with sails any more.'

'There ain't many left, that's for certain. She's getting on in years, but she'll get us to where we want to go, have no fear.'

'What's she called?' asked Ludwig, watching the great white sails flapping in the wind.

'*The Kamaria*', said the Captain. 'She's a picture ain't she?'

Ludwig nodded.

'Come on, let's get you on board.'

Ludwig joined the rest as they climbed the gangplank. The Captain was last, still grinning at the sight of his ship.

On deck, Ludwig watched the crew line up. The Captain inspected them one by one before sending them off to their jobs.

A short while later, the crew carried out their final preparations and the Captain stood near the ship's wheel. He called out to heave anchor and soon the *Kamaria* slowly started pulling away from the dock. Ludwig watched as they left Beacon behind.

'I'm sure you'll be back,' said the Captain. 'Don't worry about that. This'll all be over soon.'

'I hope so.'

The Captain gently moved Ludwig around so he was now facing the rest of the ship. 'Now, as you're still part of my crew, I've got a few things for you to do...'

Chapter Thirteen:

The Future is a Foreign Country

That evening as the sun was disappearing into the sea and the lanterns were being lit, Ludwig, tired after his day of pulling ropes, leaned against the side of the ship and watched the coastline roll by. Below him, he could see creatures swimming with the ship. Every once in a while a dolphin would come up for air.

Across the water was Galleesha. It had taken most of the day to reach it but now it felt almost within touching distance. The landscape was darkening, but every so often a cluster of lights would shine out, shimmering on the water as the *Kamaria* passed a town.

'We'll be there soon,' came a voice behind him.

'Matilda?' said Ludwig quietly.

'Call me Grandmother, dear,' she replied as she stood next to him and put her hands on the railing.

'Grandmother...what's going on? I don't understand anything, about you, about father...' He stared into the water below him.

'Don't be embarrassed. You weren't meant to know. Your father is very clever and knows how to deceive people very easily. He's done it to me enough times.'

'Why is he doing this?'

'I'm not quite sure,' replied his grandmother. 'But it may have something to do with when he was young. When Mandrake was a boy, younger than you are now, we lived in Castle Guggenstein until his father was murdered.'

'Grandfather was murdered! That's terrible!'

'He didn't tell you about that either? No, I suppose he wouldn't. Yes, your grandfather, my husband, was killed when your father was very young. By a Galleeshan spy we think. Mandrake was devastated by the loss, as was I.'

'What happened?'

'A man pretended to be someone he wasn't. Louis trusted him and the man betrayed him. Mandrake knew him too. He thought they were good friends. It was as simple as that.'

'What happened afterwards?'

'We couldn't stay in the castle any more, it was too painful. We moved to a small town in Ekharle where we owned a house. Mandrake took a long time to recover from what happened, and part of me thinks he never did. He seemed so happy in Little Wainesford, and all that went away.'

'Grandfather's death? Is that why he's doing this?'

'I think it has something to do with it, but not everything. When he was about your age he went off to school. I saw him in the holidays, but he got more and more distant while he was away and spoke to me only rarely. He wasn't unkind, just distracted, like something was always on his mind. As he got older, he left for university and that was the last time I saw him. I heard things now and again, but nothing much to speak of. Then, one day, I received a letter out of the blue saying he was going to be expelled. I left immediately, but when I arrived at the university to take him home, he was already gone. He had vanished completely. I tried to track him down, but I couldn't find him for years.'

'Why was he thrown out?'

'He had always dreamed of being a scientist like his father, and even at a young age he was thought of as very talented. But at university he started doing things that were... wrong in many ways. When his father died, it seems a part of Mandrake died with him. He did whatever he pleased to whomever he pleased. When the university found out, he was told to leave.' Matilda looked out over the sea.

'Since then, I've been trying my best to keep an eye on him. He's moved around a lot, working for anyone that will give him enough money to carry on with his experiments. Some time ago, I tracked him down to Juleto; but before I could meet him, something happened. I think he released something that killed most of the people in the town. After that, the war was just starting with Galleesha, and I think Pallenway were the highest bidders for his services.'

'The things we built. The Harvester, the seed cannon...'

'Weapons,' said Matilda.

Ludwig felt sick. He had helped make those things. He *enjoyed* it.

'I didn't even know he was back in Castle Guggenstein until Arthur Shawlworth sent me a letter asking me why I hadn't visited. I couldn't believe he was living back there after all that had happened. And that's when I heard about you as well. I was shocked to hear Mandrake had a son. But...these things happen I suppose. The rest I'm sure you can guess. I employed the Captain, Viktor and Arthur Shawlworth to keep their eyes open. When you and Hephaestus escaped, Viktor was at the castle. He told the Captain what had happened and he picked you up. The rest you know.'

Ludwig stood in silence.

Behind them, there was a ringing of a bell and the crew who had been on deck began to walk below. She placed her hand on Ludwig's shoulder.

'Come child. Let's eat.'

Chapter Fourteen:
Galleesha

Three days later, Ludwig looked up from his chores to see a town loom into view. It was old and shambling, full of rickety wooden buildings and a long, rotting dock stretching into the sea with a few fishing boats tied to it.

'Where's that?' he asked a sailor next to him.

'Kelijo,' the sailor replied.

Ludwig watched as the *Kamaria* headed to the dock.

When the ship finally came to a rest, the Captain, Hephaestus and his grandmother wandered up to him.

'Let's go mates,' said the Captain.

When they were off the ship, they walked along the dock and into the town. The streets were quiet as they continued further in. Once they got to the town square, Matilda stopped.

'Where is he?' she muttered.

Ludwig looked around and caught sight of a man leaning against a wall staring at them.

'Grandmother...' whispered Ludwig, tugging at her sleeve.

'Oh, good, he's here,' said Matilda. She stepped past her grandson and walked up to the man. They quietly exchanged a few words and then Matilda beckoned the party over.

As he went to his Grandmother, Ludwig jumped as a loud screech echoed through the town. 'What was that?' he asked.

'The train,' said the Captain. 'There's a few running

on this continent, even to a backwater like this.'

'Is that how we'll get to Galleesha?' Ludwig wondered, suddenly excited at the prospect of traveling by train for the first time.

'No dear, the railway will be too dangerous,' said his grandmother. She turned to the man Ludwig had seen. 'Sebastian here says our coaches are nearby. No one will pay attention to another few carriages on the road.' She turned to the rest of the group. 'There's no reason to dawdle,' she called out. 'We will leave straight away.'

As the carriages set off, a small, hunched beggar sitting in the corner of the square got up and walked out of the city in a different direction. As the beggar walked away, those near him or her (for it was difficult to say which) turned their heads and wondered what was making that strange, high pitched noise.

Throughout the day, they travelled past the towns and villages that stood between Kelijo and Galleesha. The towns and villages were quiet, as if an unhappy shroud was draped over them. The people Ludwig saw had none of the joy he knew from Little Wainesford.

By the evening, they came to the border. There, Ludwig woke to find a few small sheds; two painted, wooden barriers; and a few bored looking guards slouching against the shed walls in the gloom. The guards looked up at the carriages as they pulled to stop and the closest walked over.

'Wait here,' said Dr Angelus behind Ludwig. 'There can be trouble at times.' He got up, stepped out of the carriage and walked over to the guards.

Ludwig watched as the guard's faces fell. 'My lord!' said one in a strange, thick accent. 'If we had known it were you–'

'Don't worry sergeant, you are just doing your job,' replied Dr Angelus. 'Admirably, I might add. We'll just pass through if you don't mind and we'll speak no more about it.'

'Of course, my lord, of course!'

The guard stumbled back to his post and ordered the others to pull up the barrier.

Dr Angelus returned to the carriage.

'My lord?' said Mr Shawlworth as the doctor got inside. He turned to the brothers. 'Looks like there's more to our friend here than we thought!'

Dr Angelus said nothing and Mr Shawlworth chuckled. The doctor laid back as the carriage began moving again, pulling his hat over his face, but Ludwig was sure he caught sight of the doctor winking at him as he went back to sleep.

Four days later, after the party had traveled through miles of countryside (and stopped at remarkably well-prepared inns), Dr Angelus nudged Ludwig awake.

'Look over there,' he said, whispering into Ludwig's ear.

Ludwig peered out as the carriage reached the top of a hill. Dr Angelus pointed over his shoulder. Below them, in the middle of a valley, was a great, vast, sprawling city.

'Lutentio,' said Dr Angelus.

Like Beacon, it was massive, but where Beacon had smoke stacks, Lutentio had spires. Where Beacon had houses cramped together, Lutentio had gardens and parks. Buildings of white stone gleamed in the sunlight and a bright blue river split the city in two.

'Thankfully the war hasn't got this far,' said Dr Angelus.

Ludwig didn't reply, he just stared as the carriages entered Lutentio's paved streets. When they passed its citizens, Ludwig listened closely and heard them speaking with the same accent as he had heard at the border.

The coaches continued on and they eventually entered a wide courtyard. They stopped and Ludwig followed Dr Angelus outside. He looked around and saw a huge building towering up to the sky and reaching out in both directions in a curved arc. A great staircase on its front led to a massive set of doors, and on each step, bright, peacock-like guards stood perfectly still. Those at the top looked like toys from this distance.

When everyone was out of the carriages, the man called Sebastian spoke. 'Please wait here, the Superbus will be with you shortly.'

Superbus?

Ludwig watched Sebastian go up the stairs and stop in front of the massive doors. Ludwig had to squint, but after a few seconds, he saw the doors open a little way and a man stepped out.

He was short and bearded and dressed in loud robes that flew out around him as he came down the staircase, chatting merrily with Sebastian.

When they got to the bottom, Sebastian turned to the group. 'Lady and Gentlemen, may I introduce the Superbus of Gallesha, Illentine the first.'

Ludwig's mouth fell open.

A broad smile quickly spread across the Superbus' face. 'Viktor!' he cried out in the same accent Ludwig had heard on the streets. 'It's good to see you again.' He grabbed Dr Angelus and patted him hard on the back.

Dr Angelus laughed. 'Illentine, I hope you've not let Lutentio fall apart too much while I was away.'

'Only a bit, little brother,' replied the Superbus. 'But so far no one has complained.'

Little brother? The man who had helped clean the animals' cages in the Captain's circus is a Superbus' brother?

Illentine let go of his brother and went up to Ludwig's grandmother. He bowed and kissed her outstretched hand. 'Matilda, it's good to see you. It's been too long.'

'It has, Illentine,' she replied. 'But I intend to make up for that now, although I wish it were under better circumstances.'

Illentine frowned. 'We live in troubled times, my dear, but that mustn't make us unhappy.' The Superbus then turned to the Captain, Ludwig and Hephaestus. 'And who might these be?' he asked, eyeing the trio.

'This is the Captain of the *Kamaria*', said Matilda.

The Superbus raised an eyebrow. 'Captain of the *Kamaria* you say? I thought he was hanged years ago if memory serves.'

'Not me, M'lord,' replied the Captain smoothly. 'I've never been hanged. I would have remembered.'

'Really? Well... I must have heard wrong.'

'Must have, M'lord.'

Before they could continue, Matilda quickly interrupted. 'And *these*, Illentine, are my grandsons, Ludwig and Hephaestus.'

'Grandsons? Not Mandrake's surely!'

'It appears so.'

'By Azmon! That *is* a turn up for the books!' The Superbus held out his hand for Ludwig to shake.

Ludwig, worried he might do something wrong, barely touched the Superbus' hand.

'You're... you're a Superbus?' he managed.

'Indeed! Although, it's just a title. We Galleeshans are traditionalists at times.' He pointed to the top of his head.

'No crown, see? I was elected instead. Far more sensible, but not so much fun. If I try to do anything too stupid, people knock on my door and next thing you know I'm looking for a new country to live in (and possibly my head). And call me Illentine, my boy. I've enough people calling me "Superbus", I don't need another.'

Ludwig just stood there, unable to think of anything to say.

'Well... good man,' said Illentine, extracting his hand from Ludwig's and leaving the young boy alone. He moved on to Hephaestus, but took a step back to take him all in.

'I would shake your hand, but I fear I may loose it in yours!' Illentine cried. Instead, he bowed deeply. When Hephaestus did the same, the nearest guard lurched forward. Illentine laughed and waved them back.

'I don't suppose you're looking for a job are you? I'm certain you'd be *very* useful around here.'

'I–' stumbled Hephaestus, but got no further as his grandmother spoke.

'Illentine, don't tease the boys, they've had enough to deal with already. Besides, we must talk, and before that, I need a bath desperately. We've been traveling for a long time.'

'Of course Matilda. The water is boiling already.' He turned and walked back up the stairs, beckoning them to follow. 'This way, this way, let's get you all comfortable. My house is your house and all that.'

Ludwig watched the man as they climbed the stairs. Then he went over to his Grandmother. 'You know the Superbus of Galleesha?' he asked in awe.

'Of course dear,' replied Matilda. 'He's my nephew.'

Later on, after Ludwig had bathed and put on the comfortable new clothes that had been laid out for him, he left his new room to find the others in the vast palace.

For the past hour, he had paced around his room distracted and agitated. *Nephew*, his Grandmother had said. That means the Superbus and Dr Angelus were his relatives. He couldn't believe it.

Outside, Ludwig found a guard standing next to his door. He wasn't paying Ludwig any attention and stared straight ahead at the wall across the corridor.

'Excuse me,' said Ludwig, quietly.

The guard looked down briefly and then quickly looked back as if he hadn't heard anything.

'Hi,' Ludwig tried again, a little louder. 'Hey, over here.'

This got the guard's attention.

'*Sah?*' he said uncertainly.

'I need to find Illentine–' Ludwig saw the guard's face wince and corrected himself. 'I mean the Superbus. Could you tell me where is he?'

'*Sah, his lordship is in the Art of War Room, sah!*' answered the guard.

'Thank you,' said Ludwig, and not wanting to disturb the odd man further, he headed off in search of his new family. However, as soon as he turned the corner, he came to a corridor that disappeared into the distance with people rushing about between hundreds of doors. Ludwig turned around and quickly went back to the guard.

'Where... er... is the Art of War Room, exactly?'

'*Well!*' cried the guard. '*You need to go down that corridor there, turn left, follow that corridor 500 paces, go down the staircase, then at the bottom, turn, right, then right again. Continue down...*'

Ludwig stared at the guard. He didn't bother to let him finish. 'Thank you,' he muttered under his breath, and went back into the maelstrom that was the Superbus' palace.

After getting completely lost far too many times to count, and asking anyone he saw for directions whenever he could get their attention, Ludwig finally managed to find where he was meant to be.

In one part of the palace was a great hall. At the far end was a large pair of ornate double doors, and behind them, he had been told, was the Art of War room. He opened one of the doors and stepped inside. Beyond, Ludwig spotted Illentine behind a grand desk. He was talking to Sebastian and they spoke in hushed voices.

While they talked, Ludwig looked around and quickly understood why this place was given its name. The room itself was a large cylinder, reaching perhaps all the way to the top of the palace. On its walls were images of ancient battles that spiralled upwards. Taking a closer look, Ludwig realised that the paintings were moving. Each soldier depicted on the wall was walking or running or fighting or doing all manner of things. He stared hypnotized while the little soldiers battled each other, over and over. When he tore himself away, he found Illentine staring at him.

'Hi,' he said.

'Ludwig,' said Illentine, sounding serious. 'I don't know how to tell you this...' his eyes darted to Sebastian. 'Something has happened...'

'What is it?'

Illentine took a deep breath. 'Your father has invaded Beacon. I got a report a few minutes ago. We don't know what happened but by the sound of it he just marched in and took over with those machines of his. No one could do a thing about it.'

Ludwig was silent for a few moments.

'He'll attack Galleesha with the HELOTs,' said Ludwig miserably. 'He hates you, well, Galleesha I mean. I heard him say so. He was so angry when Sir Notsworth told him the war was coming to an end.'

'HELOTs? Is that what he calls those machines?'

Ludwig nodded.

Illentine frowned. 'How did he make so many so quickly? There were hundreds of them by all accounts.'

'They could be taught to make themselves,' said Ludwig, remembering the lessons he had given the first. 'The first can be taught to make the second, then those two make two more. It wouldn't take long.'

Illentine looked horrified. 'Then we must do something soon.' He turned to Sebastian. 'Send word to our generals. I must speak with them immediately. If what the boy says is true, Mandrake will come for us soon enough.'

'Yes, sir,' replied Sebastian.

Illentine bent down. 'Thank you, Ludwig. Stay here. You'll be safe. We'll stop your father, don't you worry.' And with that, the Superbus turned and left.

'Wait!' Ludwig cried after him. 'What just happened?'

'We're going to war,' replied Sebastian.

Chapter Fifteen:
Version Two

An hour later, Illentine declared war and the palace was even more chaotic.

While the city prepared, Ludwig and Hephaestus found themselves with nothing to do. Ludwig sometimes visited the museums, parks and galleries with his grandmother, while Hephaestus stayed indoors and read in the Palace library, but soon enough both brothers became bored.

Then one day, Illentine asked the brothers if they could spare a few moments. He took them down a long passageway and up a stairwell. At the top, a door opened, and they found themselves in a garden that looked out over the city. It was full of trees and flowers, and strange animals wandered about.

'I come here to think sometimes,' explained Illentine. 'But feel free to use it when you like, if you need to get away from it all.'

The brothers thanked him and watched as the Superbus walked away.

He looked as if he had a heavy weight on his shoulders.

That evening, while the brothers were in Illentine's garden watching the sunset, Ludwig yawned and turned to his brother. 'I'm going to bed now.'

'I'll stay for a while,' replied Hephaestus. 'I'd like to see the city at night.'

Ludwig nodded and set off back towards the door to the palace. As he neared the door, he saw a glowing spot hung in the darkness. Smoke swirled.

'Captain?' Ludwig called out cautiously.

'Hello, mate,' said the Captain stepping out of the shadows.

'Is anything wrong?' asked Ludwig.

'No. I just needed some air. Come on, I'll walk yer back to yer room.'

The pair left the garden and walked down the winding corridors, chatting to each other about Lutentio.
When they arrived back at the apartments, Ludwig said good night and watched the Captain stroll off down the corridor. He closed his door, turned the key, and walked over to the wash basin to begin clearing away the day's grime.

But as he lent over the water…

CRASH!

Glass few across the room. Ludwig covered his face and waited. When the glass finished falling, he looked up. On the other side of the room a hole had appeared where the window once was. Outside he could see something moving. It was the head of a HELOT.

Ludwig scrambled towards the door as strange, dull thuds echoed into the room. He quickly glanced back. The HELOT coming up through the window was very different from the one he had built with his father. As it stepped into his room, Ludwig saw eight long, metal legs coming out from underneath its body, ending in nothing more than sharp, cruel-looking points. Each time it took a step closer, the tips sliced into the ground.

Ludwig scrambled to the door, desperate to get away, but the machine shot forward, launching itself across the room and knocked him down. Ludwig twisted onto his back but the HELOT was on top of him straight away; its legs smashing down and surrounding him like a cage.

'No!' he shouted, lashing out at the legs, but he quickly pulled his hands away again as a streak of blood appeared across his palm. They were so sharp.

There was a banging on the door. The handle rattled and Ludwig looked up.

'Ludwig!' came the voice of the Captain. 'What's going on in there? Open the door!'

'Stay back!' Ludwig called out, but before he could shout again, he was hit with the dull side of one of the HELOT's legs.

A shot rang out and the bedroom door flew open. The Captain came in.

'Be careful!' cried Ludwig, groggy from the HELOT's blow.

'Stay down, boy!' The Captain raised his other pistol and Ludwig covered his ears. There was an almighty roar as the pistol went off.

The HELOT staggered back as the bullet hit. Its legs dancing across the floor, trying to balance.

Ludwig was free. He dived out of the machine's way, sliding under the bed as its sharp legs hammered down around him. He peered out from under the skirting. The HELOT was nowhere near as damaged as the others had been when they had been shot at the circus. He could see where the bullet dented the metal, but there was no hole. And it was still moving.

The machine righted itself and turned to the Captain.

The Captain cursed as he tried to get his pistols open, but before he could reload, the HELOT jumped.

Ludwig watched in horror as the machine took off and brought its front legs up in the air. It came crashing down, its legs plunged into the Captain and knocked him flat, pinning him to the ground.

The Captain bellowed and struggled, then went limp.

'No...' whimpered Ludwig.

The machine turned to him. Ludwig stood up but didn't run. There was no use.

In the corridors of the palace, Hephaestus found guards running everywhere, panic painted upon their faces as alarms blared out.

As a guard passed, Hephaestus grabbed him and brought him close. 'What's going on?' he boomed, lifting the frightened guard off the ground by his shirt.

'There's been an attack! In the apartments! Someone's been hurt!'

'No...' Hephaestus dropped the stunned man and ran.

He rounded the corner to the apartments. 'Ludwig!' he bellowed when he saw his brother's bedroom door wide open and guards going inside.

'Let me through!' Hephaestus pushed the guards out of the way, knocking many to the ground.

Inside he saw the shattered window and glass everywhere. Near the door, the guards were silently huddled around something on the floor. He could see blood pooling around their feet.

'No!'

He began pulling the men out of his way. 'Ludwig, please!' bellowed Hephaestus. But when he managed to get past the guards, it wasn't Ludwig he found.

'Hephaestus,' whispered the Captain. 'It got him, I'm sorry.'

Chapter Sixteen:
An old 'Friend'

Ludwig woke to find the ground rushing below him. He craned his head and made out the legs of the new HELOT shearing into the ground, gouging the earth as it ran. He turned his head some more. It was still night time and he had no idea where he was. But before he could say or do anything else, the new HELOT noticed its prisoner was awake and the world went away again.

When Ludwig came to again, he groaned and pressed his hands against his head. He could feel a bump beginning to rise. He went to stand up but came crashing down as his head smashed into something hard. In more pain than he had ever known, he opened his eyes and looked up. Above him were iron bars. Startled, he quickly looked around and found himself in a small cage big enough for maybe a large dog at best. He could sit up, but that was it.

When the pain started to fade, he understood he was on a ship. He could feel its gentle swaying.

Beyond the bars of his cage, two of the ordinary HELOTs stood watch.

'Water,' he croaked at them.

Neither HELOT moved. Moments later there was a creaking nearby. At the end of the room a trapdoor opened in the ceiling and another machine entered. It came over to Ludwig and placed a mug of water on the floor near the cage.

Ludwig snatched the mug and drank greedily.

'More,' he said afterward, wiping his mouth and holding out the mug. The machine took it and left the way it came in.

Later, as Ludwig drank his second mug, he heard the same dull, thudding noises he had heard in his room in Illentine's palace. He looked up towards the trapdoor. It opened and the strange new HELOT came down. It strode up to the cage and Ludwig edged back as its bladed feet hit the ground near him. Finally, the machine lowered itself down.

Ludwig watched the HELOT and the HELOT seemed to watch him. He noticed the machine would twitch occasionally, its mechanisms whining. It didn't move like the other HELOTs. They were rigid, like clockwork soldiers. This one was more like an animal. It turned its head slightly this way and that, twitching as if it were sniffing for something. Ludwig had a feeling his father had done more to this machine than just give it a different body.

'He's been busy,' Ludwig said in between gulps, trying to sound braver than he felt.

A metal plate just below the HELOT's head rippled. Ludwig saw thousands of tiny pin-heads move up and down. They began to form themselves into words.

"MORE THAN YOU CAN IMAGINE," it read.

Ludwig jumped. 'You can *talk?*'

"YES."

Ludwig tried to clear his head.

'Where are you taking me?'

"BEACON. YOUR FATHER WANTS TO SPEAK TO YOU."

Ludwig peered closer. 'Do... do you remember who you were?'

"YES."

'Can... can all of you remember?' he felt sick.

"NO."

Ludwig was relieved. 'Why only you?'

The machine stared at him.

"I'M DIFFERENT. SPECIAL."

'Who are– were you?'

The machine didn't answer.

Suddenly Ludwig's shoulders sagged and he stared at the ground. 'I'm… I'm sorry,' he whispered.

"WHY?"

'For helping make the first of you. I didn't know.'

The machine's front legs slammed into the floor inside the cage right next to Ludwig's hands. Its face touched the bars. Ludwig scampered away and pushed his back against the cage. He looked at the machine fearfully. 'What are you doing?!'

"I WAS A MONSTER BEFORE YOUR FATHER GOT ME," said the machine. "BUT THE PROFESSOR HAS SHOWN ME THE LIGHT. HE'S <u>IMPROVED</u> ME. NOW, I HAVE PURPOSE…"

Its front legs lifted off the ground and rubbed together, making an awful grinding sound like the noise of a butcher's knife being sharpened. "NOW, I'M SO MUCH MORE… AS IT WERE."

Ludwig's mouth fell open. He recognised those words. *As. It. Were.* They had stayed with him for months and kept him up at night.

'Jack?' he whispered.

Chapter Seventeen: The Bargain

'Please gentlemen, let us have some order,' Illentine called out over the hubbub in the Art of War room. 'We will get nowhere if you carry on like this.'

He stood behind his desk. In front of him were his ministers crowded around, and along the back wall were Hephaestus, Matilda and Mr Shawlworth.

The ministers all spoke at once, but after a few more pleading requests and a threat, the room hushed.

'Ludwig's kidnapping is terrible,' Illentine continued when they had settled down, 'and I am deeply concerned for him, as you all are. This attack has–'

'We don't care about the boy!' called out one minister angrily. 'What about the rest of us? The Professor could come and take us, kill us–'

The minister realised the room had fallen deathly silent. Those around him were looking just over his head. He looked down and felt very alone when he saw a large, dark shadow covering the part of floor on which he was standing.

'*Your* safety?' said Hephaestus, quietly.

'Well, I mean to say, I... we... are very concerned about your brother, young... er... man, but there are others who may be considered more important–'

Hephaestus leaned so close the minister could feel the giant's breath on his neck. 'Not to me,' he rumbled.

The minister closed his eyes tight.

'Hephaestus,' Illentine called out sternly. 'Please, leave the honourable gentleman alone. He's not thinking properly, are you minister?'

The minister looked as if was about to argue, but then thought better of it and shook his head furiously.

'No, no, of course. It has been such a trying time…'

Hephaestus stepped away and the minister's shoulders sagged with relief.

'As I was saying,' continued Illentine 'This attack has shaken us, but it hasn't changed anything.' The Superbus looked at Matilda, Hephaestus and then Mr Shawlworth. 'I'm sorry, but we can't do anything for Ludwig right now. The threat to Galleesha is a more pressing matter. Everything must focus on that. We have to prepare.'

'You can't do that!' roared Hephaestus.

'There's no reason to think he's in any immediate danger,' replied Illentine.

'No immediate danger?' said Mr Shawlworth. 'That would depend on your definition I suppose.'

Illentine sighed with frustration. 'Mandrake isn't planning to harm him. He wouldn't have made so much effort to get him back if he were. We know that much at least.'

'It doesn't matter! We can't let him have Ludwig!' cried Hephaestus.

'I wish we could do more, my boy,' replied Illentine. 'But we can't. I need everyone I've got.'

Hephaestus was about to argue some more when the Art of War room's doors swung open. Dr Angelus stepped in. He looked tired and his clothes were bloodstained.

'Viktor,' said Matilda. 'How is he?'

Dr Angelus looked at the group wearily. 'It's not good. Whoever took Ludwig, seriously hurt the Captain. I don't think he'll survive the night.'

Matilda looked down sadly. 'Oh, let him live,' she muttered. Mr Shawlworth quickly went to her, comforting her as best he could.

'I– I can help him,' Hephaestus said quietly.

'What's that?' said Illentine.

Matilda looked up through her tears.

'I can help him.'

'How lad?' asked Mr Shawlworth.

'The HELOTs, Father's machines. He didn't design them. I did.'

The room was silent for a time.

'Why in Azmon's name didn't you say something before?' cried Illentine.

'I couldn't, I didn't want Ludwig to know.'

'Hephaestus, you should have never kept this from us,' said his grandmother.

'But if Ludwig were to find out… I don't know what he would do…' Hephaestus stared at the floor.

Matilda walked over to her grandson. 'My dear child,' she said sympathetically, raising a hand to his cheek. 'You have been through too much. Ludwig would never blame you. He understands that all this is your father's doing. Trust him as he trusts you.'

Hephaestus looked down at his grandmother and nodded silently.

'You can put the Captain in one of those machines?' asked Mr Shawlworth. 'But won't he be just a slave like the others?'

'No. He would be free to do as he pleases. It would still be him in all but his body.'

'We can ask him ourselves,' said Dr Angelus. 'I can keep him alive for long enough.' He then turned to leave.

'Wait,' said Hephaestus. 'I have one condition. You have to help me rescue Ludwig. You must promise me that. I'll let the Captain die if you don't.'

'How can you-?' began Illentine angrily.

'Say "yes", Illentine,' said Matilda weakly, taking

Hephaestus by the arm and leading him to the door. 'You would do the same thing if it was Viktor, you know that. Come, let us speak to him.'

The Superbus huffed and then nodded.

'Fine.'

They walked out, leaving the ministers staring at each other, not knowing what to say.

Chapter Eighteen: Reunion

Ludwig didn't see Jack again for the rest of the voyage. He heard him walking above (the sound was unmistakable), but it was the two other HELOTs who were the only ones to keep him company. Although a third would sometimes come, bringing food and water.

Then, one morning, Ludwig was lurched awake as the side of the ship banged up against something hard. He looked up and saw the trapdoor at the top of the stairs open. Jack came down, and then one of the other HELOTs walked over and opened the cage at a nod from the spider-machine.

When Jack got to Ludwig, his plate shimmered.

"Come with me."

Ludwig stepped out of the cage and climbed the stairs. Jack followed close behind. When they got to the deck, Ludwig looked around. They were at Beacon docks. It was deserted. The ships that he had seen coming and going before sat idly tethered without their crews.

Suddenly Ludwig felt a sharp pain in his back as Jack pushed him.

"Move."

'I'm going, I'm going,' replied Ludwig

Near to the ship was a carriage with four HELOTs harnessed to it. It would almost have been comical if Ludwig didn't know what was inside them.

"Get in."

Ludwig stepped inside and the door closed behind him. He sat down, but jumped up again as Jack's legs pierced the carriage. The bladed legs moved upwards, leaving holes where light shone through. Moments later, Jack settled on the roof. Ludwig sat back down and they left.

Out of the carriage window, Ludwig saw Beacon had become a very different place to the one he left only a short time before. Every street he passed was empty. Occasionally he saw a few HELOTs walking in a slow procession or a person peering fearfully out of a window, only to vanish behind a curtain as soon as he caught their eye.

After a short while, the carriage stopped and the door opened. Ludwig stepped out. In front of him stood a massive iron gate with huge, high walls on either side. The buildings around him were dark and dirty.

'Where are we?'

"BEACON PRISON."

Ludwig stood with Jack as the gates to the prison swung open. As they parted, his father came striding out with a great smile across his face.

'Ludwig! My boy! It's wonderful to see you!' called Mandrake.

Ludwig was too stunned to say anything. After all that had happened, to see his father smiling and looking... *happy* was too much.

'I see you need time to adjust,' said Mandrake to his open-mouthed son. 'No matter. Come along, I've lots to show you.'

Ludwig tried to speak, instead all that he managed was a grunt as Jack prodded him hard in the back.

'As you can see,' said Mandrake as they walked through a courtyard full of barred windows. 'Things have changed since we last spoke, but for the better I might add. I've converted this place to the main factory, producing approximately fifty HELOTs a day. Admittedly that's not as many as I would have hoped, but it's early days.'

They stepped through the main entrance and up a

staircase to a gantry overlooking a huge hall. Below, a long production line of HELOTs was making new copies of themselves over and over.

'Incredible isn't it?' said Mandrake proudly.

'It's *horrible.*'

'Oh, come now, don't be like that.'

Ludwig remembered the empty docks and streets. 'Is…is this where all the people from Beacon are?'

'Ah, I see that secret is out. Your brother needs to learn to keep quiet. But don't be silly, boy. I was simply keeping them off the streets while you were travelling here. Some of the good citizens of Beacon are not as accepting of their new ruler as I would have hoped, and there have been a few…accidents. Don't worry, no one is here who doesn't deserve to be.'

'How can you do this?'

'Quite easily. You know how quickly they learn. It didn't take much to organise them. This place practically runs itself–'

'I meant–'

'I know what you *meant,*' said Mandrake irritably. He turned to Ludwig and frowned. 'It's for the best, Ludwig, you must understand that.'

'You're killing them!'

'No boy, that's one thing I am certainly *not* doing. If anything, I am making them almost immortal. Come with me.'

Ludwig was led to the end of the gantry where a makeshift office was set up. Mandrake picked up one of files that were spread out over a desk.

'Read it.'

Ludwig opened the file. It was about one of the prisoners. It listed his crimes. Ludwig shuddered as he read. The man it described had done truly awful things.

'He's an example of whom I am converting,' said his father. 'There are more like him, and many even worse. I have the proof right here. These creatures were a plague on humanity. Take Jack for example. You know how bad he was, now he's a productive member of society, my society. Just like the rest.'

'What about Mr Pewsnitt, or Bernard? Were they a plague?'

'Bernard? How did you... of course, Arthur Shawlworth. I'm disappointed *he* would turn on me like that.' Mandrake waved his hand dismissively. 'No matter. Yes, I converted them, but it was purely out of necessity, don't you see? Mr Pewsnitt was my first attempt. He was a sacrifice for the good of mankind. I wished there was another way but I couldn't see one. The same goes for the rest of the village. I know it must sound cruel, but in the long run they will achieve more in their conversions than they would have had they remained in their ordinary bodies.'

'How can you say that?'

'I know the arguments, boy, I've had them with myself often enough. But people when left to their own devices do not do well, not well at all. This is just the first stage of my plan. It's painful, change always is-'

'Not for you,' said Ludwig.

Mandrake turned and struck his son across his face. Ludwig fell to the floor. His cheek burned from the blow. When he looked back he saw rage in his father's eyes.

'How *dare* you!' Mandrake shouted. 'You have no idea what I've lost, child. I have given everything to do what I must! To finally rid humanity of its failures-' Mandrake paused, looking horrified, then dropped to the floor.

'Oh my boy. I'm so sorry! There's too much pressure. I didn't want to hurt-'

Ludwig didn't wait to hear the rest. He lunged forward, desperate to grab his father, to do something that would stop all this. But Jack was too quick. His legs shot out and Ludwig crashed into them, knocking the air out of his lungs and tearing his clothes. He crumpled winded back down on the floor.

Mandrake walked to his son and touched him on gently on the cheek. 'I'm sorry we have ended up like this, I really am. I never wanted it to turn out this way...' He stood up and turned to Jack. 'Please, take him away.'

Chapter Nineteen:
A New Home

Jack pushed Ludwig back along the gantry and then through the courtyard and out of the great gates. Outside, he guided Ludwig back into the carriage.

When the carriage stopped again, Ludwig found himself in one of the richer parts of Beacon. Well-kept trees lined the streets and rosebushes grew in small front gardens. Peeking over the rooftops, he could see the Superbus' palace and the cathedral's two spires close by. In front of him was a light brown town-house with a pillared entrance.

"YOU WILL STAY HERE," said Jack

Ludwig walked up the steps. The door to the house opened and behind it a HELOT stood waiting. Ludwig turned back to Jack.

'What now?'

"STAY. THE MACHINE WILL LOOK AFTER YOU."

Ludwig walked inside and slammed the door behind him. Then he turned and listened. When he heard Jack thump back onto the carriage and ride off, he tried to open the door, but it held firm. He was locked in. Behind him, the HELOT was standing still with a piece of paper in its outstretched hand. He read it.

Ludwig,

Welcome to your new home. I know it isn't the castle, but I think it will suit you well enough. The kitchen is well stocked, and a library can be found upstairs that should suffice for your continued studies. Furthermore, there is a rather pretty garden in the rear that you should make use of weather permitting. If there is anything further you require, feel free to ask the HELOT I provided.

Unfortunately, because of the recent problems between you and I, I cannot trust you to wander about Beacon on your own. However, if you tell the HELOT that you have somewhere in particular you would like to go, perhaps something can be arranged. It is an interesting city and I would not want to deprive you of enjoying it.

I will try to call in on you when I can but urgent matters of state are taking up a great deal of my time.

I look forward to seeing you soon.

- Your loving father.

Ludwig read the letter again and then scrunched it up into a ball and threw it into a corner. Afterward, he found the kitchen, sat at the table, and put his head in his hands. He looked up when he heard the whining sound come into the room.

The HELOT stood waiting.

'Go away,' Ludwig commanded.

Chapter Twenty:
A New Captain and A Stroke
of Luck:

'Captain?' said Hephaestus. 'Can you hear me, Captain?'

'Zzzzzzzzzzzzz.... Heph.... zzzzzzzzzzzzz,'

'Try again, come on.'

Hephaestus stood over a long workbench in the room Illentine had given him. On the bench was a machine. He bent down to turn its screws and change its wiring.

'Hephaestus...... zzzzz...... I can hear you.... zzzzz..... but you're.... far away.. zzz... mate.'

Hephaestus tightened a loose fitting and smiled. 'How's that?' he asked.

'Better,' said the machine.

'Now try opening your eyes.'

The Captain's eyes whirred slightly as the lenses focused.

'I... zzzz.... I can see you! By Azmon, you're ugly!' Hephaestus bashed the Captain in the chest playfully. 'It looks like you're working,' he replied, stepping away from the table. 'Can you move you arms? Just think about it. Imagine you're moving them.'

Hephaestus watched as the Captain's arms shook, then rose slowly from his sides.

'Now,' continued Hephaestus, 'let's see if you can walk.'

On the first morning in his new home, Ludwig was woken in his (admittedly) very comfortable, new bed by the sound of voices outside. He got up, opened his bedroom window and looked out into the street. Below him, people and carts were going about their business. It was pleasant to see them. It was almost normal. He'd half expected to wake to a ghost town.

Then he looked further down the street and his heart fell. He saw a group of HELOTs coming towards his new home. When the people below saw them, some ran while others just stood by quietly, not daring to move. They all looked terrified. As they passed by Ludwig's room, he saw one was carrying a gramophone. It was winding the mechanism slowly and sending a message out in a voice Ludwig recognised.

'Citizens of Beacon,' it said.'Do not be alarmed.   My name is Professor Mandrake von Guggenstein, and I am currently looking after Beacon and Pallenway. The council has failed you, good people, and I am here to put things right. Do not be afraid of the machines. They answer to me and are here to keep the peace. Please go about your lives and everything will be well.'

Ludwig looked at the "good people". They didn't look convinced. He closed the window and looked around the room. On a chair, his clothes were neatly pressed and cleaned. The HELOT most have put them there. He shuddered, imagining it creeping around his room while he had been sleeping. He got dressed and went downstairs.

On the ground floor, he opened the door to the back garden and went outside. It was a small, cheerful place with bright flowers lining the edge of the lawn. Bees buzzed, collecting pollen and looking content. Ludwig envied them.

On the lawn was a chair and a table, both basking in the warm sunlight. Ludwig was about to sit down when the garden wall caught his eye. On it, thick vines crept up. He remembered how he had escaped from his room that very first time all those months ago and laughed. Then he called out to the HELOT standing by the door.

'Fetch me a glass of orange juice,' he ordered, trying to calm his voice. The machine walked inside and left him alone.

As soon as it had gone, Ludwig jumped up and ran to the far wall. He grabbed the creepers and hauled himself up to the top, then he swung his legs over and dropped to the other side. When he hit the cobbled ground below, he looked around and found himself in a small alley. One direction carried on past more houses. The other opened up onto a larger street where he saw people passing by. He ran towards them.

At the end of the alleyway, between two high buildings, Ludwig caught his breath and peered out into the street. It was crowded and he could easily hide himself among the people. He looked both ways, and after making sure no HELOTs were marching by, he stepped out into the traffic.

On the road, he tried to keep his pace slow, but he found his legs wanted to go faster all the time. His heart was pumping hard in his chest. As he continued on, a thought struck him.

He had no idea where he was going!

After an hour of walking, Ludwig stopped on a street corner. Nothing looked familiar.

What was it the Captain said? The lick Street runs all the way through the city...

Ludwig quickly caught the attention of the next person who walked by.

'Excuse me, please! Excuse me!'

The man's eyes darted to Ludwig. 'What is it? What do you want?'

'I'm looking for Thelick Street, sir. Which way is it, please?'

'You don't know?' said the man, surprised.

Ludwig shook his head.

The man took a step closer. 'You're not from around here are you lad? Oh, you've picked a bad time to visit Beacon and no mistake.'

'It wasn't my fault.'

The man suddenly smiled. 'No, I doubt if it was.' Then he pointed into the distance, his voice gentler now. 'Thelick street is that way. Just follow this road and you'll come to it.'

'Thank you!' said Ludwig, walking off in a hurry.

The man watched him go. 'Much good it'll do you,' he said sadly.

As Ludwig walked on, he suddenly spotted a group of HELOTs coming down the road. Terrified, he dived into the next alley he saw and pushed his back against the wall. Peering round, he watched the machines slowly march past. When he could see them finally walking away, he relaxed. But before he could step back out onto the street, he heard dull thumps behind him and a high-pitched whine. His shoulders sagged and he dropped to the floor.

Jack's plate shimmered. "DID YOU REALLY THINK IT WOULD BE THAT EASY?"

'I see yer got a little carried away with the decoration,' said the Captain as he stared at himself in the mirror. He twisted and turned to get a better look at the metallic hulk that was his new body; the mechanisms inside him whirred and adjusted. He gleamed from the polish and his motors sounded smooth and capable.

Hephaestus knelt behind him and made some final

alterations. When he was finished, he stood up and smiled at the Captain's reflection. 'What would have you preferred? Flowers?'

'I don't know, mate. The swirls I can live with, used to those all my life, but the skulls seem a bit much.'

The Captain was now as tall as Hephaestus and just as broad. His chest and back were covered in plates of bronzed metal, and his new jagged head poked out of the top. At the places where his arms joined his body were two skull-heads cast in the same metal as the rest of him. The Captain tapped them and looked at Hephaestus.

'I thought they'd suit you,' said Hephaestus. 'You know... because of your past. They'll strike terror into the hearts of your enemies.'

'I look ridiculous,' muttered the Captain and Hephaestus tried not to laugh. 'Come on, let's get this over with.'

The two of them left Hephaestus' new workshop and walked down the palace corridors. Occasionally they would pass a guard who would stare wide-eyed as the Captain stomped by.

'I don't think a single one of them managed a proper hello,' said the Captain when they reached the doors of the Art of War room.

'I imagine you come as a bit of a shock.' replied Hephaestus. He looked at the door and drew breath. 'Ready?'

'I could murder a cigar,' said the Captain. He started to pat down his body out of habit.

'You've got no lungs,' said Hephaestus. 'No mouth either come to that.' He took out a handkerchief and wiped the smudges left by the Captain's fingers.

'I'm starting to regret lettin' yer do this,' said the Captain, knocking away Hephaestus' hand. 'Stop fussing.'

Hephaestus put the handkerchief away, stepped forward,

and pushed open the doors.

Beyond, everyone was standing by Illentine's desk, deep in conversation. When they heard the door open they looked up.

'Captain?' said Matilda as the two strode in.

The Captain bowed low at those assembled and laughed. 'Aye, Matilda. It is.'

'Is it really you?' she cried, running over to the man-machine.

'As much as me as he could salvage,' replied the Captain, pointing a mechanical thumb over his shoulder at Hephaestus.

'Incredible!' said Illentine.

'Amazin',' said Mr Shawlworth. 'How does it feel?'

'Strange, but not so bad. It took a while to get used to, but now I barely remember its not my own. Until I see a mirror that is.'

There was a cough from Hephaestus.

'Don't worry, we haven't forgotten,' said Illentine, stepping back behind his desk. 'The rescue. We already have a few ideas.'

'Thank you,' said Hephaestus.

'Right…' began Illentine.

Chapter Twenty One:
The Dead Speak

The next evening, Illentine's train pulled into Kelijo. Hephaestus watched from the carriage window as Illentine's soldiers got off the train and spread out over the platform, moving a few people away. Moments later, they were met by other guards dressed in bright purple.

Hephaestus stepped off the train and watched as Illentine walked up to a guard and spoke with him.

'Something's going on,' Hephaestus said to the others when they joined him.

Illentine walked over to Hephaestus and the others. He looked worried. 'We've had some very disturbing news. You'd better come with me.'

They followed Illentine through Kelijo's decrepit side streets. Guards stood every few meters looking nervous. Soon, they turned into another alley and Illentine opened a grimy-looking door.

The building they entered was a guard-house. Soldiers in uniforms stood up from their work when Illentine entered. Some saluted as he walked by. The Superbus nodded and greeted them quietly.

Hephaestus saw these men looked worried too, and it wasn't because of the Captain or himself (although some did edge away when the Captain went near them). They looked tired, like fear had been gnawing on them for hours

They carried on through the guardhouse and were led down a flight of stairs. Below were the cells. As they walked, Hephaestus noticed the inmates looking up and whimpering fearfully when the caught sight of the Captain.

But they aren't surprised by the sight of him...

'Here we are,' said one Illentine's guard.

Hephaestus looked inside the last cell. It was dark, but against the far wall he caught a glint of metal.

Oh no...

'You *caught* one?' gasped Dr Angelus.

'Don't worry, it's been restrained,' said the guard grimly. He took his lantern and aimed it at the far wall.

A HELOT stood at the back of the cell. Its feet were covered with cement in a solid block and its arms and body were bound against the wall with heavy iron chains. It was perfectly still, but Hephaestus heard the quiet hum that meant it was still working.

'It tried to get away,' continued the guard. 'We lost ten men stopping it.' He bit his lip. 'But we brought it down in the end. It just stopped struggling. We did all that-' he pointed at the cement and the chains. 'Just in case.'

'Can I go in?' asked Hephaestus.

The guard hesitated and looked at Illentine.

'Let him,' replied the Superbus. 'Be careful, Hephaestus.'

The guard unlocked the cell and moved aside.

Hephaestus opened the door and everyone held their breath as they watched him slowly walk up to the HELOT. He edged closer, one step at a time, wary of the machine, but it did nothing. When he was only a short distance away, he leaned forward.

Suddenly the HELOT lurched at Hephaestus. Its arms shot forward but stopped short of the giant as the chains in the wall held. The noise was terrible, and in the other cells the inmates wailed and screamed to be let out.

Hephaestus fell back, crashing into the floor and scrambling towards the cell door. He caught his breath and saw the HELOT throwing itself forward again. Its legs stayed in the cement, but the brickwork where the chains were bolted to the wall began to crack.

On its third attempt, the chains came away. The machine crashed down. Then it looked up and threw its claws into the floor.

Hephaestus looked on in horror and the HELOT began to crawl slowly towards him, it legs still in the concrete. Before he could do anything, he felt something cold on his neck. The Captain grabbed him by his collar and hauled him back out of the cell in one quick pull. Hephaestus' weight was almost nothing for the Captain's new arms. The Captain then stepped past him and walked into the cell.

The Captain reached down, took hold of the HELOT and lifted it up. The machine tore at him, trying to find something to rend. It flailed wildly, and an awful screeching echoing through the cells as its claws scrapped down the Captain's body. But the Captain was too strong. He smashed the HELOT into the wall as hard as he could. Then he pulled it back. It was crushed and dented but still struggling. He was about to smash it again when Hephaestus called out to him.

'Don't!'

'What?' the Captain cried back, surprised. He quickly ducked as the HELOT tried to tear his eyes out.

'We can use it,' said Hephaestus, getting up off the floor.

'If you say so.'

The Captain took hold of one of the machine's arms and twisted. The motors wailed as they broke. After the first arm came away, he took the other and did the same. Then he let go and the HELOT hit the floor, rocking back and forth, still trying to fight. Finally the Captain kicked it into the corner and walked out.

'Captain-' said Matilda, rushing up to him. She touched the marks the HELOT had left on his body.

'Have you killed it?'

'It ain't alive, Matilda,' said the Captain quietly. The rest watched the HELOT squirming on the floor like a helpless animal.

'Illentine,' said Hephaestus, 'can you send someone to your train?'

'Of course.'

Hephaestus walked over to the HELOT and picked it up. 'Tell them to bring my things here. I want to talk to it.'

'Do you really think this will work?' asked Matilda, peering over Hephaestus' shoulder.

Everyone was standing in the guardhouse crowding around Hephaestus. The HELOT was propped up in front of him on one of the desks. Next to it was a strange machine he had taken from his luggage.

'What's left of the mind inside the machine is basically a recording device,' Hephaestus explained. 'So I think I can tap into it. We may be able to get something that'll help us.'

He opened the HELOT's head, reached inside, and when he withdrew his hands everyone around him leaned forward. In his palm was a cube that flickered and shone with bright light.

'What is it?' asked Dr Angelus.

'Its brain,' replied Hephaestus.

He rested the cube down on the desk and took two wires that were attached to his machine. 'Now, if I just...' He placed the wires onto the cube. His machine spluttered and fizzed before going quiet again.

'Hello?' said Hephaestus. 'Can you hear me?'

The machine made odd noises, but little else.

'Hephaestus-' said Dr Angelus, but before he could

continue, he was interrupted by a new voice.

'I can hear you,' said the machine. It was a woman's voice. Hephaestus cried out in shock and Mr Shawlworth gasped.

'I know that voice!' said the gardener. 'By Azmon, that's Mrs Pewsnitt!'

'Hephaestus, must you do this?' asked Matilda. 'I knew Mrs Pewsnitt well. I can't… You must destroy it.'

'Let's wait outside,' said the Captain, gently trying to guide Matilda away, but she wouldn't move.

'No. I'll stay. I should hear this.'

'It may have been Mrs Pewsnitt once,' said Hephaestus. 'But it isn't any more. I'm sorry, but I have to know if I can get anything from it. It may help us find Ludwig.' He turned back to the cube. 'HELOT,' he said. 'Tell me your orders.'

Everyone leaned closer to listen as the machine spoke.

'One,' it began in Mrs Pewsnitt's voice. 'Explore Kelijo. Two: find locations for HELOT production. Three: remain hidden. Do not let anyone identify HELOT before returning home. Four: protect Ludwig von Guggenstein. Five: kill anyone who interferes with all previous orders. Six: if all other orders cannot be achieved, shut down and await further orders.'

'HELOT production?' said Illentine. 'It's worse than I thought.' He turned to the guard closest to him. 'Sergeant, send word to Lutentio. Tell them that Mandrake's machines may be in our cities. Tell them to keep their ears open and investigate if they hear anyone's gone missing. Get them searching for HELOTs too, and for Azmon's sake tell them to be careful! Then pass on word to our neighbours. Mandrake's probably going after other countries beside Galleesha.' The guard saluted and ran out the door. Illentine turned to the others. 'Mandrake is using our own people to build his army. This *cannot* happen.'

'We should get to Beacon as fast as we can,' said the

Captain. 'But at least we know Ludwig's safe.'

'I'll go back to Lutentio,' replied Illentine. 'I'll arrange my armies from there. Matilda, come with me.'

Everyone nodded and began to leave the guardhouse. As they left, Hephaestus unhooked the wires from the cube and picked it up again.

'Goodbye Mrs Pewsnitt,' he said quietly, before crushing the cube in his great fist.

After they had said their goodbyes to Matilda and Illentine, Hephaestus, the Captain, Dr Angelus and Mr Shawlworth climbed up the *Kamaria's* gangplank. As they stood on deck, a hushed silence descended over the ship. The crew stared at the new Captain.

'Greetin's mates!' He cried out, much to their surprise. 'I know I look a bit different now, but but it's still me, your good, old captain.'

The crew shuffled their feet, but said nothing.

'… And if we're not movin' in the next five minutes, the first person I lay my lands on will be in the bilge before they can blink! And when I lay my hands on someone they'll feel it!'

The crew stared at the man-machine. Then one sailor lent over to another and whispered, 'I'm pretty sure that *is* the Captain. I'd recognise that threat anywhere…' The other sailor nodded. Soon all the crew we muttering and agreeing that the metal man was indeed who he said he was.

'Now!' the Captain bellowed.

The crew ran to their jobs, almost falling over one another.

The Captain turned back to Hephaestus. 'Right, that wasn't too hard. Come on lad, let's find you a bunk.'

Chapter Twenty Two:
An Unexpected Visitor

The days passed slowly after Ludwig had tried to run away. He would get up late and go to bed early. He would eat, but didn't care what food was put in front of him. Between meals he would stare out of his bedroom window and watch the people go by. He did little else.

That was until...

One night, while Ludwig was asleep, the front door opened and someone entered the house. The stairs creaked as the stranger made their way upwards. The bedroom door opened and the stranger stood by Ludwig's bed.

'Ludwig?'

'Mhmm,' replied Ludwig. He didn't wake up.

'Ludwig! Get up!'

'Eh–?'

'We need to go!'

Ludwig opened his eyes. Standing over him was a very familiar face.

'Notsworth?'

'Yes boy!'

'Notsworth! What are you doing here?'

Notsworth quickly put his hand over Ludwig's mouth and pressed his finger to his own. 'Shhh lad! What do you think I'm doing! Rescuing you of course!'

Ludwig jumped out of bed and threw on his clothes.

'Wear this as well,' said Notsworth, handing Ludwig an oversized coat from his bag.

Quietly, they left Ludwig's bedroom and started down the stairs. Ludwig was about to speak when Notsworth pointed down. In the flickering light of the lamps, the HELOT left to watch over Ludwig was standing facing the hallway wall like a naughty child. They crept onwards and passed the machine. It didn't move.

'How did you get it to do that?' asked Ludwig.

The older man didn't reply. Instead, he opened the front door and they stepped out into the night. Ludwig shivered despite the thick coat.

'I thought Jack was watching me?' said Ludwig.

'Jack?'

'The spider HELOT.'

'That monster's been distracted for the evening.'

Notsworth pointed over the roof tops and Ludwig could see a glow. Something was burning.

'It'll be back though,' Notsworth continued. 'We mustn't dawdle.' He led Ludwig down some streets to where a carriage was waiting. The driver watched them but he was silent as Notsworth opened one of its doors.

'Get in, lad.'

Ludwig jumped in. Notsworth followed, and the carriage moved off.

'How could you tell the HELOT what to do?' asked Ludwig as they turned on to Thelick Street.

'Your father gave me command over them.'

Ludwig jumped back. 'You work for father?!'

'Don't worry lad! I'm on your side!'

'You mean-'

'Do you really think I would sneak into your house in the middle of the night and whisk you away if I was helping him?'

Ludwig shook his head.

'I'm glad we have that sorted. Your father asked me to

help him and I, well, *couldn't* say no. But I hate what he's doing my boy and will do everything in my power to stop him!'

The big man looked at Ludwig to make sure he understood. Then he laughed and patted Ludwig on the back. 'Ah, it's grand to see you lad!'

'You too Notsworth.'

'So what have *you* been up to? Your father said you'd disappeared.'

Ludwig told Notsworth all that had happened. The big man listened fascinated.

'You've had an interesting time and no mistake. I'm sorry you're caught up in all this, I really am–'

Suddenly there was a knock on the carriage roof.

'Stay down!' Notsworth hissed and pushed a startled Ludwig onto the floor.

Ludwig looked up and saw Notsworth's face. He was terrified.

'It's just me,' called Notsworth out of the window. 'I'm heading home for the night.' There were footsteps outside, then the carriage started off again.

'Sorry, lad,' he said afterward. 'I forgot about the checkpoint. Mandrake's got them up on all the roads going out of Beacon. No one gets out.'

Ludwig looked back and saw two HELOTs standing by the road leading into the city.

'Where are we going?' he asked, turning back.

'My estate,' replied Notsworth.

A short while later, Ludwig and Notsworth turned off the road surrounded by fields and along a path that led down a tree-lined avenue. Eventually the coach came to a stop and they got out.

'Welcome,' said Notsworth cheerfully.

Ludwig stared up at the house before him. It was massive, stretching off either side of the main entrance with rows of large windows pouring light onto the lawns and driveway. Ludwig could only guess at the number of rooms within, it must be well into the hundreds.

'Come on lad.'

Notsworth stepped out of the carriage and Ludwig followed him inside.

Inside, the manor seemed to be stuffed with strange objects. They were hung from the ceilings, displayed on tables or simply piled up on corners. Ludwig was about to pick one up when he heard a growl from the next room. He looked up to see Notsworth being knocked to the floor by a great black and white tiger.

'Abberati!' The big man cried, grabbing the cat around its neck and pulling her down with him.

'Oh, hello Notsworth,' came a voice behind the tiger. 'I'm terribly sorry. She heard you come in and I couldn't keep the old girl from greeting you. A successful evening, old chap? Fancy a snifter by the way?'

Abberati stepped off Notsworth, and he lifted himself from the floor. Ludwig looked past him and saw a man standing there. He was dressed in a suit and had his hair plastered down flat. His face was sharp, but not unkind.

'And hello to you too!' the man called out with a wave when he saw Ludwig. 'You must be the lad Notsworth was going on about. How do you do?'

Ludwig gave a wave. 'Well…'

'Sorry, Ludwig,' said Notsworth. 'This is Georgios Torosidis.' he turned to the man. 'Georgios, let me introduce Ludwig von Guggenstein.'

The man's eyes lit up. 'Its really him, Notsworth? Oh excellent! Wait a moment will you?' And just like that, he quickly ran off without another word.

'Sorry about him,' said Notsworth. 'He's a good chap, but a few palm trees short of an oasis if you know what I mean.' Notsworth patted his cat, who was purring at his feet. 'Abberati, this is Ludwig, say hello won't you.'

The great tiger swished her tail and padded over to Ludwig. When she got close enough she nuzzled her head against his hand.

'Go on, scratch her around her ears, she likes that.'

Ludwig did as Notsworth said. The massive cat rolled her head around Ludwig's hand and then let herself drop on the floor. Ludwig followed her down, stroking her soft fur. He started laughing and hugged the animal tightly. Then he looked up to find a small group of men and women standing watching him.

'Ladies and gentlemen,' called out Notsworth. 'This is Ludwig. He is my guest and you will treat him like he is your own flesh and blood.'

The group, a strange-looking bunch, each gave short greeting. They looked as if they were studying him closely.

Ludwig went over to Notsworth and tugged on the big man's sleeve. 'Who are they?' he asked quietly.

'These are my faithful companions, my boy!' beamed Sir Notsworth. 'Each one has helped me innumerable times on my adventures.'

Notsworth lent close to Ludwig. 'A while back I needed a bit of help getting out of a jam and this lot was here to help. Unfortunately that was a few years ago and now I can't get rid of the blighters. But Abberati likes them and they don't cause any trouble, so where's the harm,' Then in a louder voice, 'Oh yes, fine companions! Loyal to the core! Come! Let us feast!'

Then there was a loud cheer from the group as Ludwig was led to the dining room.

That evening, while Ludwig devoured his food, he listened as those in Notsworth's employ chattered around him. Occasionally, one would raise a glass to Ludwig if they caught his eye. Ludwig did the same and smiled, not knowing what else to do. Next to him sat Sir Notsworth. The big man bombarded Ludwig with questions about all that had happened to him.

'I didn't feel brave,' replied Ludwig as he wiped his mouth and took a sip of the water by his plate. 'I was terrified most of the time.'

'Perhaps, lad,' said Notsworth. 'But to walk away from your father like that took courage. Most would have gone back to him in the end, no matter what.'

'If it wasn't for the Captain finding us, I might have done. I hated being in those woods.'

'You need to introduce me to this Captain,' said Notsworth. 'He sounds like an interesting fellow.'

Ludwig looked down. 'I– I think he's dead. When Jack came...'

'Oh my boy, how awful.'

Notsworth clasped a hand on Ludwig shoulder sympathetically. 'When this is over, I'll have a statue built in his honour. How about that?'

Ludwig felt a lump in his throat. 'What about you?' he asked, trying to change the subject. 'What happened when Father attacked?'

'Ah,' said Notsworth. 'That's a story in itself. But I wouldn't want to bore you,' replied Notsworth

'Go on,' said Ludwig, 'Tell it.'

'Oh, yes!' roared Sir Notsworth's companions. 'Tell it! Tell it!'

'Oh, if I must," sighed Notsworth. "Well, I was in Beacon at the time, you see. I was sitting in a hotel room when I heard screams coming from the street. I know Beacon can be a bit… dangerous at times, but it was rare to hear someone cry out the way *they* did. So I went over to the balcony and peered about, and what I sight I saw! Marching up the street was row upon row of your father's machines. It was madness. People were fleeing in every direction, trying to get away. They must have thought it was the end of the world and Okana's own demons were stalking the earth!'

'What did you do?'

'I was about to make a run for it when there was a bang at the door. I opened it and there stood a HELOT in all its glory. I quickly ran back, grabbed a chair, and was about to clobber the diabolical thing when I saw it was holding a note in its hand. The note told me to follow the HELOT, to the old Superbus' Palace, and it was signed by your father. So I did, and inside, I found your father. Surprised, I went up to him and asked him what in blazes was going on.'

Notsworth paused and looked at Ludwig sympathetically. 'Ludwig, I think your father's gone stark raving mad, and that's the long and short of it.'

'I know,' said Ludwig glumly.

'He kept going on about his "vision". He said that since we had been friends for so long, he wanted me by his side at this "incredible" time. I thought I might be able to do something about him if I kept on his good side so I agreed. This was only a couple of weeks ago but it feels like years! We've been trying to do something about your father ever since but, in all honesty, we haven't had much success so far. Getting you back has been our first real victory.'

'How did you find out about me?'

'Merselda here,' Notsworth gestured to one of his companions, 'Said she saw a young boy being taken into the prison by that odd-looking HELOT. She followed you when you came back out again and found the house where I got you. When Merselda described the boy she had seen, I just knew it was you.'

'Won't father suspect you now I've gone?'

'I imagine he'll think you're roaming the street of Beacon if he's doing any thinking at all.'

'Thank you Notsworth.'

The big man smiled. 'Don't mention it my boy.' He then stood up and raised his glass in the air.

'Ladies and gentlemen,' he called out. 'Allow me to introduce the newest member of the Freedom Fighters of Beacon, Ludwig von Guggenstein!'

The others stood up raised their glasses.

'Hip, hip–' began Notsworth. But before he could finish a huge cheer rang around the hall. Everyone ran over to Ludwig, picking him up and carrying him around the mansion in an antique chair. They cheered as they threw him up into the air.

A few days later, Ludwig sat on the veranda and watched Notsworth's companions playing cricket on the lawn. It was coming to the end of summer and the air was still warm and the trees still green. He took a sip of his juice and snuggled down into the cushions on the sun lounger. Abberati lay at his feet curled up, asleep and undisturbed by the shouts from the game.

There was a noise behind him. He turned and saw Notsworth. He looked concerned.

'What's wrong?' asked Ludwig.

'Perhaps nothing my boy. At least nothing to do with you I hope. I've received a message from your father.'

'What did he say?'

'A ship's been spotted off the coast. He wants me to see what it's up to.'

'That doesn't sound too bad.'

'Not for you, but for the poor souls on that boat it's a different matter.'

'Why?'

'That spider HELOT isn't the only new design Mandrake's come up with.'

Chapter Twenty Three: Overboard

On the third day of sailing, Hephaestus was laying on his bunk below deck reading. As he turned to a new page, there was a shuffling nearby. He looked up. Mr Shawlworth was there. The old gardener nodded a greeting and sat down.

'We'll be near Pallenway soon, lad,' he said. 'I thought you might want to come up on deck to see it.'

'In a bit, I want to finish this first.'

Mr Shawlworth stood up and turned to go, but then paused and looked back at Hephaestus. 'We'll find him, you know.'

Hephaestus looked at the gardener.

'I know,' he said. Then he got up and put the book away with his other belongings. 'Wait. I will come with you.'

On deck, they found the Captain gleaming in the sun and staring out over the sea.

'Ahoy there!' He called out when he saw Hephaestus and Mr Shawlworth.

Hephaestus waved back, and as he started to walk over to the Captain there was a cry from the crow's nest.

'Land hoy! Land hoy!'

He looked across the sea and saw Pallenway come into view.

'All right!' shouted the Captain. 'There's the bay. Prepare to weigh anchor-'

Creeeeaaakkkk!

There was a great rending sound from the side of the

ship. Water sprayed into the air, covering the deck, and the sea churned against the hull. The *Kamaria* rocked in the water.

'What going on?' cried Hephaestus.

'Captain!' cried one of the crew running out from below deck. 'Come quick!'

The Captain ran down into the ship's belly and Hephaestus and Mr Shawlworth followed. Below, they found water streaming in through small holes in the hull, and every few seconds another would appear. The crew were trying to patch them up but they couldn't work fast enough.

The Captain took one look at what was going on and ran back on deck. He lent over the side of the ship and looked down.

'I'll *kill* him!' the Captain muttered. Then he turned to the terrified crew. 'Abandon ship!'

Everyone stared at the Captain, then, seconds later, they started running. Those on the rigging and in the crow's nest raced down to the deck as the life boats started to drop into the water. As everyone got ready to leave, the *Kamaria* shook. They could feel it sinking.

'What's going on, Captain?' asked Dr Angelus.

'Looks like Mandrake's set a trap for us. I saw something movin' down there.'

Hephaestus looked over the side but all he could see was churning, white water.

Suddenly the *Kamaria* lurched to one side. Those too slow to grab on to something were flung into the water. Hephaestus watched as the men broke the surface. They started swimming towards the life-boats, but suddenly they were dragged down again. Something pulled at them. Hephaestus tore his eyes away and dived into the nearest lifeboat just as it was released. Dr Angelus and Mr Shawlworth were beside him. It dropped from the side of the *Kamaria* with a crash. Water sprayed in every direction.

'Row for it!' shouted Mr Shawlworth as soon as everyone had recovered from the fall. Hephaestus grabbed a paddle and they started rowing towards shore as fast as they could. While they rowed, Hephaestus looked around.

The Captain was still on the *Kamaria's* deck.

'Captain! What are you doing?' he cried out.

The Captain cupped his hands to his mouth. 'I ain't waterproof am I? Looks like this is as far as I go. Save Ludwig!'

Hephaestus almost laughed, then stood up and shouted as loudly as he could.

'YES! YOU ARE!'

But the Captain didn't seem to hear him.

'I think he wanted to go down with his ship,' said Dr Angelus next to him. 'He's going to have a surprise in a minute. Come on, let's go before those things-'

But it was too late.

The lifeboat rocked as something under the water smashed into its side.

When Hephaestus regained his balance, he passed his oar to Dr Angelus, and before anyone knew what he was about to do, he jumped off the boat and into the water.

'By Azmon!' cried Mr Shawlworth.

Those on the lifeboat watched in silence as the water broke and Hephaestus came up. In between his massive arms was a HELOT. It was different from the other ones they had seen before. Instead of legs, it had a great tail like a lobster, and oversized claws that had caused the holes in the *Kamaria's* hull. It thrashed wildly and slammed its tail into Hephaestus; but he held tight, crushing the machine in his arms. Soon enough, its tail stopped flapping and it went limp.

When Hephaestus was certain it was dead, he let go and

it sank into the depths. He looked up at those on the boat.

They were staring at him.

'Help me up,' he said swimming up next to the boat. But as went to climb aboard he suddenly disappeared under the waves once again.

'He can't fight all of them!' shouted Dr Angelus, pulling out a pistol and desperately searching for something to shoot at.

'Sit down and row!' shouted Mr Shawlworth, 'We're goners otherwise!'

But before an oar touched water, the crew on the lifeboat watched with their mouths open the next lobster-machine fired from the water and up into the sky. It soared over them and came down again with an almighty splash. When they turned back, they cried out as Hephaestus broke the surface.

Hephaestus clawed at the lifeboat, trying to get back on board. They pulled him over the side and he collapsed, panting, with cuts all over him.

'The Captain-' he spluttered. 'The Captain's down there.'

No one said anything. Instead, they took their oars and rowed as fast as they could. After what seemed like an eternity, the little lifeboat got nearer to shore. When they were close enough, they jumped out, desperately hoping no HELOT was nearby. They trudged onto the beach and fell down exhausted.

Hephaestus rolled over in the sand. Far away he saw the top of the *Kamaria's* mast disappear into the sea. He looked over the water and up and down the beach, but he saw no one. It looked like they were the only survivors. The rest had been taken. He looked back out over the sea and as he watched, the waves parted and the Captain's head appeared. Hephaestus jumped to his feet as the Captain stepped out of the water.

'He's made it!' cried Hephaestus. The rest of those on

the beach turned on their backs and cheered wearily.

Water streamed off the Captain as he walked out of the sea. His legs were covered in muck and seaweed and he had dents and scratches all over his body.

'Hello mates.'

'We thought we lost you,' said Dr Angelus.

'Apparently it's not that easy,' he replied, catching Hephaestus' eye. 'Where's everyone else?'

The others looked at the Captain sadly.

'Oh,' said the Captain. He was silent for a while and stared out to sea. When he was done, he turned back to the others.

'Come on, we need to leave. We've got a job to do.'

The others looked at the Captain sadly.

'I'll scout ahead,' said Mr Shawlworth quietly, breaking the silence. He lifted himself up slowly and began making his way towards the tree line.

'Wait, I'll come with you,' said Dr Angelus running up behind. The two men then disappeared into the undergrowth next to the beach.

Dr Angelus and Mr Shawlworth crept through the trees slowly, looking around and listening, checking to see if anyone was near.

'There should be a road—' began Dr Angelus, but went suddenly silent. Mr Shawlworth looked at him.

'Over there!' hissed the Doctor.

There was a noise in front of them.

Dr Angelus held out his other pistol and Mr Shawlworth took it. Then they knelt down and waited.

Seconds later, a HELOT came out of the bushes. Mr Shawlworth took aim and fired. The HELOT flew back, crashing to the ground. But that wasn't the last of it. Four more appeared, too many for them to handle.

'Run!' cried Dr Angelus.

'Stop!' Boomed a voice.

Dr Angelus and Mr Shawlworth turned and saw the four HELOTs standing completely still. They looked at each other, then over to some rustling bushes. Sir Notsworth O'Reilly burst out in front of them.

'Hello?' Sir Notsworth called out. 'Shawlworth? *Viktor Angelus?* What in Azmon's name are you doing here?'

He went over to the gardener and the doctor and shook their hands.

'It's good to see you!' he said happily. 'By Azmon, so it is! Sorry about those things' he said, pointing at the HELOTs. 'They can be a bit keen.'

Hephaestus and the Captain appeared out of the bushes. Sir Notsworth took one look at the two giants and his mouth fell open. 'Ah...'

'We heard gunshots,' said the Captain. 'Are yer all right?'

'Perhaps,' said Mr Shawlworth. He gave Notsworth a long stare. 'What are *you* doing here Notsworth, and why can you order those machines about?'

'You two know each other?' asked the Captain.

'We met a few times at Castle Guggenstein,' replied the Gardener. 'He's a friend of Mandrake.'

Notsworth pulled his gaze away from the Captain and Hephaestus and looked at Mr Shawlworth. 'I... well, Arthur, I mean to say...working for Mandrake-!' he stuttered.

But before Sir Notsworth could finish, Hephaestus grabbed him by his shirt and pushed him up against a tree.

'You work for father? Give me a good reason why I shouldn't pull your arms off!'

Notsworth suddenly came to his senses. 'What? No, you misunderstand me old chap!' He patted one of Hephaestus' massive arms. 'I'm not on his side, believe me!'

'I don't,' replied Hephaestus.

'Hang on lad,' called out Dr Angelus as he reloaded his pistols. 'Let him speak. I'll vouch for him.'

'Hephaestus?' said Notsworth, his eyes suddenly brightened. 'Hephaestus! Is that really you? I haven't seen you since you were a baby!'

'You *know* me?' asked Hephaestus, surprised.

'Of course my boy! Your father showed you to me when you first arrived in Pallenway. I remember you hiding behind his legs when he introduced you! Not so shy now, eh?'

Hephaestus put Notsworth back on the floor and stepped back.

'What's going on, Notsworth?' asked Mr Shawlworth.

'Well, it's like this...'

Notsworth explained all that had happened in Beacon since Mandrake attacked. Then he told them about Ludwig.

'You have him?' asked Hephaestus. 'Where?'

'He's back at home, safe. Come on, I'll take you to him.'

'Notsworth,' said Dr Angelus. 'How many HELOTs do you have with you?'

'Twenty, Viktor, minus those you shot. I'll send them back to Beacon. One of them will carry a message saying everyone on the boat was taken. Mandrake won't be any the wiser.'

Notsworth disappeared for a few minutes. Then the others heard the whining sounds of the HELOTs fade away.

'So Hephaestus made you?' asked Notsworth as he and those who had survived the attack on the *Kamaria* walked through his manor's front door.

'In a manner of speaking mate,' replied the Captain.

'Incredible.'

'Where is he?' Hephaestus interrupted, his eyes darting around.

'Hang on,' replied Notsworth. 'Ludwig! I say, Ludwig! Are you there?'

Moments later, Ludwig came into the entrance hall with Abberati in tow. 'How did it-' he began, but got no further when he saw Notsworth's guests.

'Ludwig!' Hephaestus cried. He ran over to his brother, picked him up and hugged him hard.

'Hephaestus?' mumbled Ludwig.

Then he saw the Captain.

'What's-?!'

'Easy mate,' the Captain replied. 'Glad to see me?'

Ludwig walked over to the Captain and touched his chest carefully. 'But how?'

He turned and looked at his brother. Hephaestus was staring at the ground. He understood in an instant.

'You did this?'

Hephaestus nodded.

'Then the HELOTs...'

He nodded again.

Ludwig was silent for while. Then he walked up to his brother and took his hand. 'It doesn't matter. Really, it doesn't. Father used you.'

Hephaestus stared at his brother. Then he let out a laugh and swung him onto his shoulders. Ludwig laughed too and looked at Notsworth.

'What do we do now?'

'Remember that prison you got taken to?' said Notsworth. Ludwig nodded. 'We're going to blow it up.'

Chapter Twenty Four:
Jailbreak

After dinner, they all sat around the dining room table discussing their plan. Ludwig sat listening while he passed Abberati scraps from his plate.

'We should be able to get past any patrols easily enough, but do we have anything to destroy the place?' asked Dr Angelus.

'I think I can help there,' said Notsworth. He left the dining room and came back a few minutes later with a leather satchel in his hands. He opened it and pulled out a large metal box. Holding the box very carefully, he placed it on the table. 'I got this from Mandrake a few years ago. For the war,' he explained uncomfortably.

Ludwig recognised it.

'I worked on that! It's for mining—' He paused. 'It's not for mining is it?'

The rest of the table looked at him sympathetically. Notsworth shook his head.

'That'll destroy the prison,' Ludwig said quietly. 'It's a Jerix device. I was told it was meant to move mountains.'

'Amongst other things,' said Notsworth.

'We should get ready to leave,' said Dr Angelus.

'Hang on,' the Captain interrupted. 'How are you going to carry it?'

The rest turned and looked at him with expectant eyes.

'No chance!'

'You would be best, Captain,' said Hephaestus. He stepped behind him. 'Imagine the left side of your back opening up, just below your shoulder.'

'What are you doing?' said the Captain cautiously.

'Trust me.'

The Captain went quiet. Seconds later, there was a click and a plate on his back sprang open, much to his surprise.

'There's enough space in here to put the bomb. All I need to do is pad it out so it doesn't bang about. You should be fine.'

'*Should?!*' said the Captain. 'Okay, fine, put it in. But you owe me.'

'So, when are going?' asked Dr Angelus when Hephaestus was finished.

'Two in the morning would be best,' replied Notsworth. 'No one will be around.'

'Other than all those HELOTs of course,' muttered Mr Shawlworth to himself as everyone got up and left the table.

Later that night, the Captain, Hephaestus, Dr Angelus, Sir Notsworth and Mr Shawlworth stood in the shadows of Beacon prison. Thanks to Sir Notsworth, they had got past the HELOTs guiding the city easily enough.

'Stand back,' whispered the Captain. He walked a few paces back from the prison wall and started running. He twisted, hunched his shoulders, and smashed into it, going straight through. When the dust and brickwork had settled, he came back out.

'Come on!'

They went inside and found themselves in one of the empty cells. They passed through the cell into the prison corridor. Only a few lamps remained lit as they edged their way forward. When they passed the other cells, they saw they were all empty.

'It looks like Mandrake's got them all,' said Notsworth quietly.

They carried on through the prison, passing from one cell block to the next.

A short while later, they came to a pair of doors. They stepped through and into a large room. Beyond, they found row upon row of HELOTs stretching all the way to the far wall. There must have been hundreds. They took one look at the machines and dived back into the hallway.

'By Azmon that was close!' hissed Notsworth.

Hephaestus cracked open the door again and peered inside. He realised they weren't making any noise.

'I don't think they're finished,' he whispered to the rest. Then he opened the doors and stepped through.

The rest followed and looked around. On one side of the room were tables full of metal cubes.

'Are they the things that make them work?' asked Notsworth.

'Yes,' replied Hephaestus.

'And each one has someone inside it...'

Hephaestus nodded gravely and turned to the rest. 'Captain, come here.'

The Captain stepped over to Hephaestus and let his back open up. Hephaestus took the device and set it on the ground carefully. He pressed a switch and a small cover flipped open. Underneath were buttons and an hourglass. He pressed a few of the buttons and turned to the rest.

'We have ten min-'

Suddenly there was a loud crash and glass fell from the ceiling. Everyone looked up, and from above, something big fell.

Jack crashed into the ground on his eight legs. He turned to the Captain and his front rippled.

"Hello Captain."

'Jack,' the Captain replied. 'Ludwig told me about what Mandrake has done to you,' He stepped warily around the machine. 'Never thought you'd end up another man's slave.' He turned and called behind him. 'Start running. I'll catch up.'

Everyone else started making their way towards the doors, but Jack skittered across the room and blocked them.

"You're not going anywhere."

Mr Shawlworth took out his pistol and fired. Jack shifted and the bullet blew a hole through the wall.

"Stupid."

Jack launched himself forward.

The old gardener tried to jump out of the way but he was too slow. One of Jack's legs caught him and pinned him to the ground. He yelled out, collapsing on the floor; but before Jack could to strike him again, Dr Angelus and O'Reilly fired with their own pistols. Jack flew back and Mr Shawlworth scrabbled out of the way.

While Jack was distracted, the Captain ran and slammed into his side. The two machines slid across the floor and the Captain smashed Jack with his fists. Jack tore back, and metal screeched and groaned. When they came to a stop, the Captain steadied himself. He quickly reached out and grabbed two of Jack's legs in each hand. Jack tried to pull away, but the Captain quickly jerked his arms upwards. There was a terrible squeal and Jack's legs bent at a strange angle. Then the Captain threw Jack across the room. Jack crashed into a wall and fell to the floor. He threw out his legs to get up, but he couldn't. His front legs had been twisted too badly. They gouged the ground uselessly.

'Get out!' shouted the Captain to the rest.

Hephaestus took one look at Jack and then turned and ran, grabbing Mr Shawlworth as he passed. Dr Angelus and

Notsworth were close behind.

'We can't leave him!' struggled Mr Shawlworth, but Hephaestus ignored him.

When the Captain saw they were safely out of the room. He ran to Jack. He brought his fists crashing down on the spider-machine. Jack tried to fight back, lashing out with his six good legs and clawed arms whenever he could, tearing great gashes across the Captain's arms and chest and exposing the pistons underneath. But Hephaestus had made the Captain too well. He grabbed each of Jack's legs in turn, twisting them as Jack tore into the Captain's body. Soon enough, Jack was a wrecked pile of metal, jerking around on the floor, unable to do anything except pull himself along slowly. Crippled.

The Captain stepped closer and Jack's plate rippled.

"CAPTAIN. DON'T."

'Don't what?' asked the Captain. 'Don't ruin your life like yer did Ludwig and Hephaestus? I knew you were a bad 'un, Jack. But to do that, to children! How could yer?'

The Captain reached out, but suddenly heard Hephaestus calling him over his shoulder.

'Captain! Get out! Now!'

The Captain looked at Jack and then the bomb.

The machine that was once Jack dragged itself across the floor as The Captain turned and ran. Jack could barely get a few feet before something broke. Then he just lay there, twitching.

Minutes later the building exploded.

Chapter Twenty Five:
It Ends

From the roof of Notsworth's manor, Ludwig and Notsworth's companions watched as a flash appeared in the sky over Beacon. They cheered loudly and slapped each other on their backs.

They did it! They really did it!

Later, Ludwig stood on the porch as Notsworth's carriage appeared in the distance. The heroes had returned. When the carriage pulled up, Ludwig and the rest clapped, but they fell silent when they saw Notsworth's face.

'Move aside,' he called to them. 'Arthur's been hurt.'

Behind him, Hephaestus and the Captain unfolded themselves out of the carriage. In their arms was Mr Shawlworth. His clothes were stained and he groaned quietly. Quickly, he was taken inside and upstairs with Dr Angelus trailing behind.

Ludwig tried to follow them up, but Notsworth stopped him.

'Let the Doctor work, lad.'

Ludwig sat himself down on the bottom step of the staircase. A few moments later, Abberati came up to him. He scratched her behind her ears and waited, not sure of what to do with himself. A short time later Hephaestus came down.

'How is he?' Ludwig asked.

His brother shrugged. 'He lost a lot of blood, but it looks like he'll live. Come on, let's get something to eat and I'll tell you what happened.'

On the first day after the destruction of the prison, the house was quiet. Thankfully, Mr Shawlworth would live.

On the second, the reports started coming in.

Ludwig listened as Notsworth's men recounted what they saw in Beacon. His father had not taken the attack on the prison well. Those living in Beacon were now being told to stay in their homes. They were not even allowed to go and buy food. They lived on handouts given out by the HELOTs.

This, said Notsworth's men, was too much for the people of Beacon. After they had all seen the prison go up, they saw that Mandrake was not invincible. They rebelled, attacking HELOTs whenever they saw one alone. Ludwig felt sick as he heard how many must have died trying to destroy the machines.

By the fifth day, it was civil war. Mandrake said he would let the people starve if they didn't stop. The people of Beacon fought back.

By the ninth day, there was no more word from Beacon. Two of Notsworth's men went to the city but they never came back.

Hephaestus pulled out a chair in the dining room and sat down. He looking at the others. 'So what do we do now?'

'We wait,' replied Dr Angelus. 'Illentine should be here in a few days. We should hold tight until then. It's desperate, but Illentine's armies can do more than we ever could right now. We'd never get into the city alive.'

'Can't we do *anything*?' asked Ludwig.

'No, mate,' said Captain. 'I'm sorry.'

'But you destroyed the prison, surely there's something...'

'We were lucky,' said Dr Angelus. 'It was easy to get into Beacon then. We slowed Mandrake down, but we haven't stopped him. We'll need an army for that.'

Those around the table got up and quietly left. Ludwig watched them. Their heads were bent down low. They were angry and frustrated that they could do nothing.

When they had gone, Ludwig went outside.

'Is that it?' he muttered to himself. 'Just wait?'

'Fraid so, lad.'

Ludwig jumped and then turned. On the veranda, Mr Shawlworth was sitting in a chair wrapped in blankets. His eyes were closed and he had a peaceful expression on his face. He voice was shaky from the concoctions Dr Angelus had given him.

'It's funny,' he mumbled. '*You* could walk in there without any of those things stopping you. '

'What do you mean?'

'Ha, you could skip down the streets and none of those things would do lift a finger! Tra-la-la! They wouldn't lay a finger on *you*.'

The old gardener muttered some more until he was too tired to speak. Dr Angelus' potions were strong.

And Ludwig started to think.

That evening, Ludwig quietly opened his bedroom door and looked out. No one was in the corridor. Dressed, he crept onto the landing, pausing next to each room to hear sleeping sounds beyond. He carried on and soon got to the main staircase. He walked down slowly, trying to put as little weight on each step as possible so as not to make them creak. When he reached the bottom, there was a noise behind him. He turned and there stood Abberati, watching him. He knelt down and the tigress padded over to him. When she was near, he took hold of her neck and pulled the big cat close.

'I have to do this,' he whispered in her ear.

Abberati purred as Ludwig stroked her. Then he got up and went to Notsworth's study. Abberati followed behind. Inside, it was pitch black, but Ludwig dared not turn on a light for fear of someone seeing. He wandered to Notsworth's desk and began opening the drawers. Soon he found what he was looking for. He stuffed the thing in his coat, then walked back to hallway, patted Abberati once more, and walked out of the front door.

Ludwig arrived in Beacon as the sun came up. It had taken hours to get there, but with any luck, no one in Notsworth's manor would be awake yet.

In front of him, the first roadblock leading into the city appeared. Fearing what the machines might do if Mr Shawlworth was wrong, he crept along the side of the road, hiding behind fences, walls and hedges. When he was close, he paused.

Please let this work…

He stepped out onto the road. The machine saw him instantly and jolted forward, then stopped, turned and went back.

It worked! They won't touch me!

He carried on, and soon the fields disappeared and he was in Beacon proper. It was hellish. Much, much worse than he had imagined. Beacon's streets were empty. Houses had windows and doors smashed in or boarded up. Occasionally, he saw things that made him choke.

He continued on into the heart of the city and came

across HELOT patrols. When they walked past, Ludwig heard his father's voice blaring out. His voice was cracked. Broken-sounding. It trembled with rage. It stuttered and sometimes made no sense. He rambled endlessly.

Ludwig walked on, touching his jacket and feeling the reassuring lump underneath. Then he looked up over the houses and saw the Superbus' palace.

He's there.

'Ludwig?' called Hephaestus, knocking on his brother's door. 'Are you getting up?' Frowning, he pushed the door and went inside. His brother's bed was empty. It looked like it hadn't been slept in all night. On the dressing table there was an envelope addressed to him. He opened it and read:

> *Hephaestus,*
> *I have gone to Beacon. Father must be stopped.*
> *I'm sorry. I hope to see you soon.*
> *L.*

Hephaestus ran out of the room. 'Notsworth!' he bellowed down the hall.

There were two more HELOTs guarding the entrance to the Superbus' palace. Ludwig ignored them.

Beyond were arched hallways full of old portraits and crystal chandeliers. On he went, climbing through the palace until he came to a set of grand double doors. He heard music playing from the other side. He opened one and went in.

'He's gone!' Hephaestus cried, running through the house.

'Calm down, Hephaestus,' said Dr Angelus, grabbing hold of the giant. The others were gathering around and Hephaestus told them what had happened.

'Oh no…' began Mr Shawlworth, but before the gardener could continue, there was a neighing of horses outside and one of Notsworth's men came running in.

'What is it?' asked Notsworth.

'Ships, I saw ships! Illentine is coming!'

Everyone looked at each other, then ran out towards the stables and into Notsworth's carriage.

Inside the palace, Ludwig found his father. He sat at a piano, with his eyes closed, his head slightly tilted, and his fingers dancing upon the keys.

Ludwig began to walk towards him, but as he got closer he looked out over the room's balcony. Far away, beyond the city and the docks, hundreds of ships crowded the horizon.

Illentine's fleet is here. I must do this now.

He reached into his jacket, pulled out the pistol and walked to his father.

'I'm sorry.'

Mandrake's eyes flew open. His arm shot out, knocking the pistol away. But he was too slow. There was a bang. A bullet tore into his shoulder, knocking him back. He hit the ground and groaned.

Ludwig looked on in horror as he dug into his pocket. He grabbed another bullet and cracked open the pistol. Meanwhile his father got up and came staggering towards him.

Ludwig pushed the pistol closed again.

'How *dare* you!' Mandrake cried, lashing out and knocking Ludwig to the floor, splitting his lip. The pistol slid away. 'I am trying to *help* you, child, don't you understand that?'

Ludwig scrambled across the ground towards the balcony and pointed out to the city and the ships.

'Are you trying to help them as well?'

'If I have to fight them, I will.'

'Why?' Ludwig asked, sobbing now. 'Why are you doing this? What did they do to make you hurt so many people? Look at Beacon. Look what you've done to it!'

His father looked over the desolate, burnt city. He waved his hand dismissively.

'Sacrifices, Ludwig.'

'Stop it! Stop saying that!'

His father bent down so his nose was almost touching his son's. His face was white. Ludwig didn't know if it was the loss of blood or the anger.

'You don't *understand* boy,' his father snarled. 'They try to destroy me. Always. Oh, they'll use me when they want, but then, when they no longer need me, they cast me aside.'

Ludwig's mouth fell open. 'All this, because they didn't want the *HELOT*?'

'And other things besides!' snapped Mandrake, his voice cracking. 'You'll see. They'll use you too. When my father died…'

'You're talking about Grandfather. Matilda told me what happened.'

'What? No. It doesn't matter.'

'He died.'

'It doesn't matter!'

'His murderer. Grandmother said you were friends.'

'Not friends…'

'He used you too.'

'And the rest! My tutors!'

'At university. You were a genius, but you were told to leave.'

'I wouldn't do what they wanted. You should have heard them, boy.' spat Mandrake. 'They can do nothing. My HELOT. It was so easy.'

'Hephaestus' HELOT.'

'Ha! He didn't know what he had created! *I* saw!'

'And this is what has become of it.' Ludwig got up, wiped the blood from his mouth and walked over to his father. He took his hand. 'Your machines in the water are attacking the ships. Look.'

Mandrake turned and watched as some of the ships began sinking. They could hear screams on the wind.

'It needs to be done,' Mandrake said quietly, his voice cracking. 'I have too much work...'

'How many lives are you prepared to take?' asked Ludwig softly. 'And they won't stop, you know. They'll fight until no one is left. When the ships land the people of Beacon will see, and they'll fight as well. Soon they'll be at the palace, and they'll make it here...'

'There are hundreds of HELOTs–'

'And there are *thousands* of them. They know about your machine in Kelijo, they know your plans. They think they are fighting for their lives!'

'That's madness, boy. All they need to do is…'

'Do what?'

Mandrake stared at his son.

'*Do what?*' shouted Ludwig.

'Submit…' whispered his father.

'Don't kill thousands because of what a few people did to you! You can save everyone if you want to. If you don't, they won't stop until you are dead. Don't you understand?'

'I can't.'

'Then I have to do this.' Ludwig reached down. There was a quiet click as Ludwig pulled his pistol's hammer back.

'Would you really kill me?' His father asked quietly. Sounding almost human again.

'If I have to.'

Mandrake reached into his pocket and pulled out a small metal box like the one he had used at the circus. He held it out to Ludwig.

'Take it.'

Ludwig edged closer but kept the pistol pointed towards his father.

'I scare you that much?'

Ludwig ignored him and took the thing in his hand.

'Speak into it. The HELOTs will do as you say.'

'What?'

'Trust me.'

Ludwig lifted the device to his mouth. 'Stop,' he commanded, feeling foolish after all that had passed.

'It's done.'

Ludwig stared at the thing in his hands. That's all it took, one word. He dropped the device on the floor and crushed it under his foot.

Mandrake turned and stared out over the city.

'I… I didn't mean for things to go this far. It just happened. The first HELOT… it seemed so easy. Hephaestus is a genius. But when they said they didn't want it… ah, it was too much! And then things got out of control. You found Hephaestus and I couldn't have you knowing what I had done. I panicked boy, you must understand that.'

What about the villagers? Were you scared of them too?'

'No, but when they came to the castle, they wanted my head! After all I had done. It was easier to…'

'Get rid of them.'

'No... but I had done too much. I couldn't turn back. I had *power*, boy. I thought, if I sacrificed a few-'

'Don't say that word.'

'Kill. Are you happy? If I killed a few, I could change things for the better.' His father slumped. 'You don't know what it's like boy, to be able change everything you saw was wrong with the world.'

Ludwig felt the pistol in his hand.

'I think I might.'

REWIRED

By Alex Keller

"There are worse people than me, boy. Much worse."

An old family, torn from power, wants to rule once again. But their heir is dead, and only one man can give them a new one: Mandrake von Guggenstein.

In the thrilling sequel to "Haywired", an old deal finds Ludwig and Hephaestus once again drawn into their father's machinations as they hunt for "Grilsgarter", a strange creature and harbinger of a nightmare future who has come to collect on their father's promises.

As the ghosts of von Guggenstein past catch up with the present, the brothers find themselves at the ends of the earth, desperate to stop a terrible war that will tear their home apart.

ISBN: 978-1-906132-34-7

UK £7.99

By Robin Price & Paul McGrory

Jemima Mallard's year has not started well. First she loses her air, then someone steals her houseboat, and now the Youth Cops think she's mixed up with a criminal called Father Thames. Not even her dad, a Chief Inspector with the 'Dult Police, can help her out this time. Oh – and London's still sinking. It's been underwater ever since the climate upgrade. All in all, it's looking like deep trouble for the girl they call 'Miss Hap'.

The story is told in words and over 70 stunning illustrations.

ISBN: 978-1-906132-03-3
UK £7.99
USA $14.95 / CAN $16.95

Get a sneak peak at some illustrations from London Deep by visiting www.mogzilla.co.uk